# THE STORY SO FAR...

*Aether is believed to be the substance of the cosmos...*

*The intrepid Claire Dulac sets out to confirm its existence.*

ARCHIBALD... IF I'M RIGHT, AND IF THE DETECTOR WORKS...THIS WOULD BE THE GREATEST DISCOVERY IN HISTORY!

BUT YOU'RE MISTAKEN, CLAIRE.

PLEASE, COME BACK DOWN TO EARTH.

*After her disappearance, her husband, Archibald, and their son, Seraphin, continue her research into aether.*

*When Claire's logbook is found, it draws the attention of powerful figures:*

*King Ludwig of Bavaria, who dreams of traveling among the stars...*

*...and Bismarck, the formidable prime minister of Prussia, who plans to conquer them.*

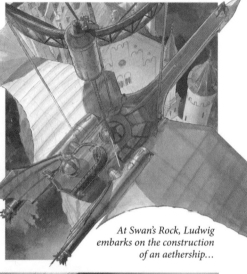

*At Swan's Rock, Ludwig embarks on the construction of an aethership...*

*But his chamberlain, von Gudden, in the service of Bismarck, plots to gain power for himself.*

*Fearing for their safety, the king, the Dulacs, and their two young associates, Hans and Sophie, flee aboard the marvelous invention, setting off on an adventure...*

*...far beyond their expectations.*

NOW OUR JOURNEY INTO THE UNKNOWN TRULY BEGINS.

*So far, indeed, that King Ludwig never returns, enthralled by an unknown lunar device that transports him to the distant reaches of the heavens.*

*Back on Earth, our heroes hide on a remote isle in Brittany, seeking to discover the secrets of the aetherite crystals they brought back from the moon. Meanwhile, in Prussia, the schemes of Bismarck continue unabated...*

ALEX ALICE

# CASTLE
## IN
## THE
# STARS

### THE KNIGHTS OF MARS

First Second

*New York*

**First Second**

English translation by Anne and Owen Smith
English translation copyright © 2019 by Roaring Brook Press

Published by First Second
First Second is an imprint of Roaring Brook Press,
a division of Holtzbrinck Publishing Holdings Limited Partnership
120 Broadway, New York, NY 10271

Don't miss your next favorite book from First Second! For the latest updates go
to firstsecondnewsletter.com and sign up for our enewsletter.

Library of Congress Control Number: 2018953554

ISBN: 978-1-250-20680-0

Our books may be purchased in bulk for promotional, educational, or business use.
Please contact your local bookseller or the Macmillan Corporate and Premium Sales Department
at (800) 221-7945 ext. 5442 or by email at MacmillanSpecialMarkets@macmillan.com.

Originally published in 2017 in French by Rue de Sèvres as *Le château des étoiles - Volume 3: Les chevaliers de Mars*
French text and illustrations by Alex Alice copyright © 2017 by Rue de Sèvres, Paris.
First American edition, 2019
Book design by Chris Dickey

Printed in China by RR Donnelley Asia Printing Solutions Ltd., Dongguan City, Guangdong Province
10 9 8 7 6 5 4 3 2 1

# *1870...*

## THE CONQUEST OF THE STARS HAS BEGUN!

**ON EARTH,** EMPIRES LOOK TO THE
HEAVENS TO LAUNCH A NEW TYPE
OF COLONY.

**THE MOON** IS A SLOWLY DYING WORLD.
YET HIDDEN ON ITS DARK SIDE IS A TOWERING
STRUCTURE THAT BEARS UNMISTAKABLE
EVIDENCE OF ANCIENT LIFE...

**VENUS.** WHAT SECRETS DOES SHE HIDE
BENEATH HER DENSE CLOUDS? HUMID AND
HEATED BY THE NEARBY SUN, DOES SHE
SHELTER PRIMEVAL PLANT AND ANIMAL
LIFE BENEATH HER OPAQUE VEIL?

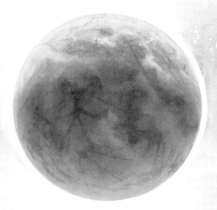

**MARS.**
THE MOST COVETED OBJECT AMONG THE STARS.
DOES IT SUSTAIN LIFE? ASTRONOMERS HAVE CLAIMED TO
SEE STRANGE LINES THAT CROSS THE PLANET'S SURFACE—
IS THIS EVIDENCE OF PAST CIVILIZATIONS?

THE KEY TO ALL THESE SECRETS BEARS A NAME:

AETHER.

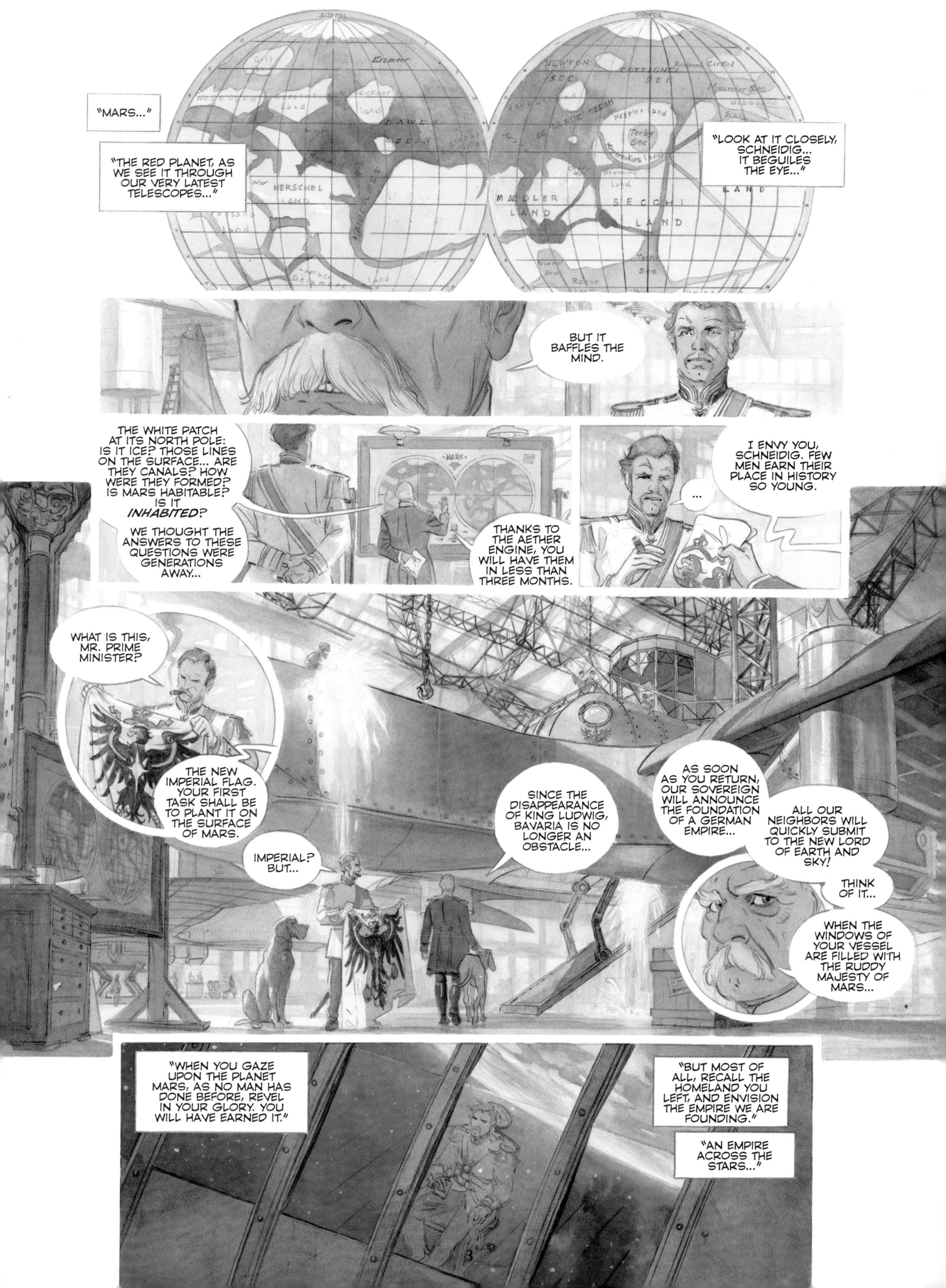

"MARS..."
"THE RED PLANET, AS WE SEE IT THROUGH OUR VERY LATEST TELESCOPES..."
HERSCHEL LAND
MAEDLER LAND
SECCHI LAND
"LOOK AT IT CLOSELY, SCHNEIDIG... IT BEGUILES THE EYE..."
BUT IT BAFFLES THE MIND.
THE WHITE PATCH AT ITS NORTH POLE: IS IT ICE? THOSE LINES ON THE SURFACE... ARE THEY CANALS? HOW WERE THEY FORMED? IS MARS HABITABLE? IS IT ***INHABITED***?
WE THOUGHT THE ANSWERS TO THESE QUESTIONS WERE GENERATIONS AWAY...
THANKS TO THE AETHER ENGINE, YOU WILL HAVE THEM IN LESS THAN THREE MONTHS.
I ENVY YOU, SCHNEIDIG. FEW MEN EARN THEIR PLACE IN HISTORY SO YOUNG.
...
WHAT IS THIS, MR. PRIME MINISTER?
THE NEW IMPERIAL FLAG. YOUR FIRST TASK SHALL BE TO PLANT IT ON THE SURFACE OF MARS.
IMPERIAL? BUT...
SINCE THE DISAPPEARANCE OF KING LUDWIG, BAVARIA IS NO LONGER AN OBSTACLE...
AS SOON AS YOU RETURN, OUR SOVEREIGN WILL ANNOUNCE THE FOUNDATION OF A GERMAN EMPIRE...
ALL OUR NEIGHBORS WILL QUICKLY SUBMIT TO THE NEW LORD OF EARTH AND SKY!
THINK OF IT...
WHEN THE WINDOWS OF YOUR VESSEL ARE FILLED WITH THE RUDDY MAJESTY OF MARS...
"WHEN YOU GAZE UPON THE PLANET MARS, AS NO MAN HAS DONE BEFORE, REVEL IN YOUR GLORY. YOU WILL HAVE EARNED IT."
"BUT MOST OF ALL, RECALL THE HOMELAND YOU LEFT, AND ENVISION THE EMPIRE WE ARE FOUNDING."
"AN EMPIRE ACROSS THE STARS..."

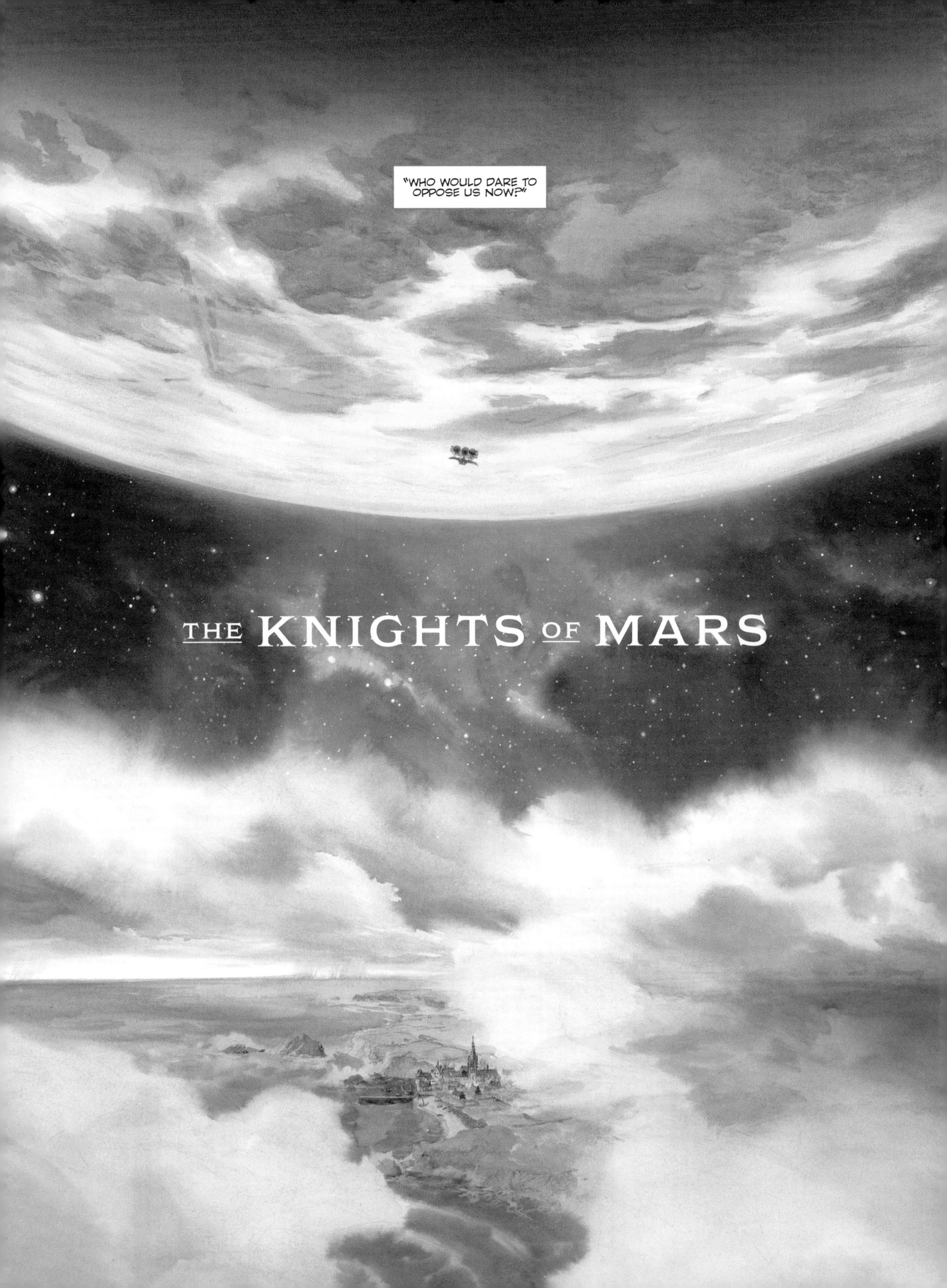
"WHO WOULD DARE TO OPPOSE US NOW?"
THE KNIGHTS OF MARS

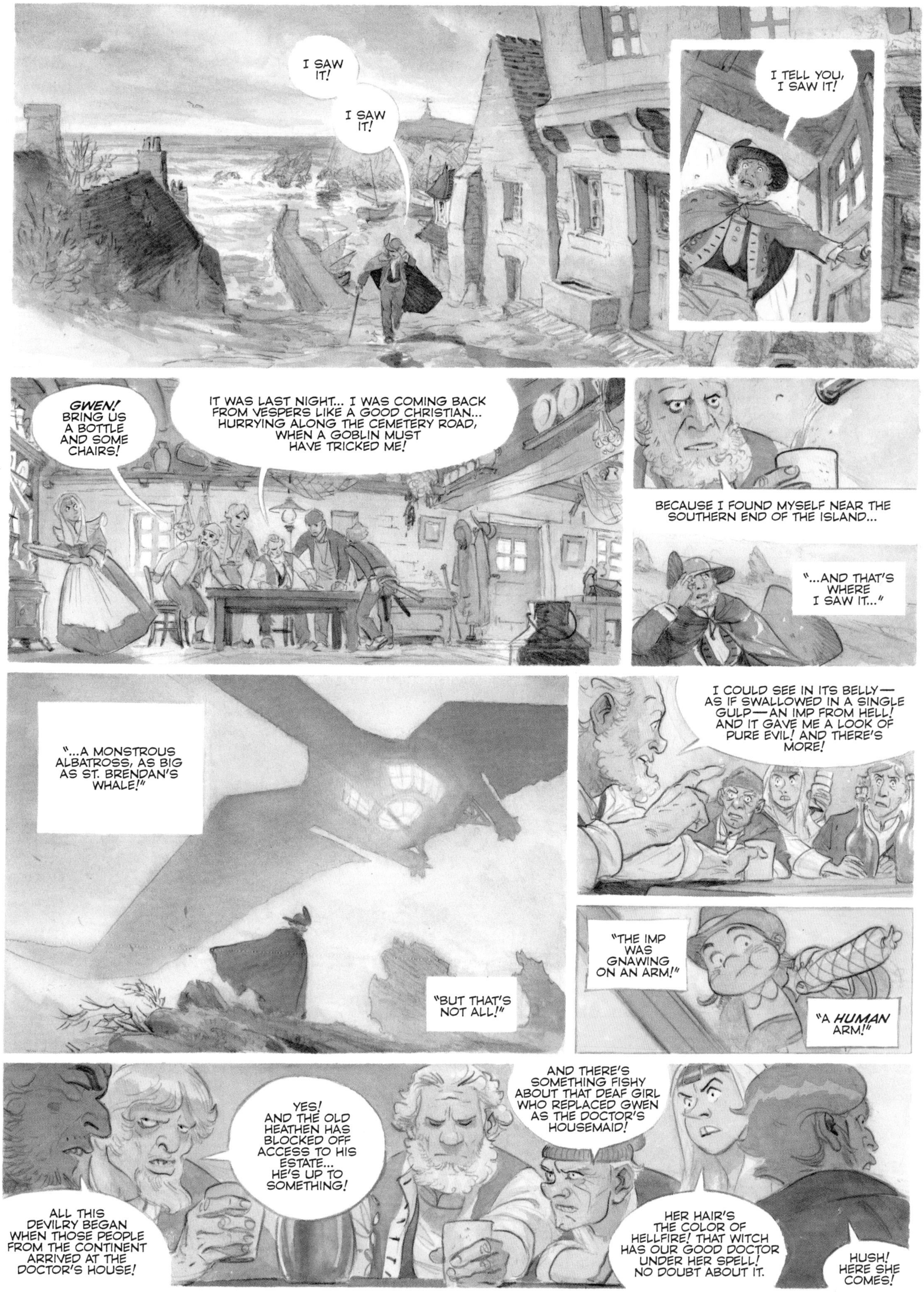

I SAW IT!
I SAW IT!
I TELL YOU, I SAW IT!
GWEN! BRING US A BOTTLE AND SOME CHAIRS!
IT WAS LAST NIGHT... I WAS COMING BACK FROM VESPERS LIKE A GOOD CHRISTIAN... HURRYING ALONG THE CEMETERY ROAD, WHEN A GOBLIN MUST HAVE TRICKED ME!
BECAUSE I FOUND MYSELF NEAR THE SOUTHERN END OF THE ISLAND...
"...AND THAT'S WHERE I SAW IT..."
"...A MONSTROUS ALBATROSS, AS BIG AS ST. BRENDAN'S WHALE!"
"BUT THAT'S NOT ALL!"
I COULD SEE IN ITS BELLY—AS IF SWALLOWED IN A SINGLE GULP—AN IMP FROM HELL! AND IT GAVE ME A LOOK OF PURE EVIL! AND THERE'S MORE!
"THE IMP WAS GNAWING ON AN ARM!"
"A HUMAN ARM!"
ALL THIS DEVILRY BEGAN WHEN THOSE PEOPLE FROM THE CONTINENT ARRIVED AT THE DOCTOR'S HOUSE!
YES! AND THE OLD HEATHEN HAS BLOCKED OFF ACCESS TO HIS ESTATE... HE'S UP TO SOMETHING!
AND THERE'S SOMETHING FISHY ABOUT THAT DEAF GIRL WHO REPLACED GWEN AS THE DOCTOR'S HOUSEMAID!
HER HAIR'S THE COLOR OF HELLFIRE! THAT WITCH HAS OUR GOOD DOCTOR UNDER HER SPELL! NO DOUBT ABOUT IT.
HUSH! HERE SHE COMES!

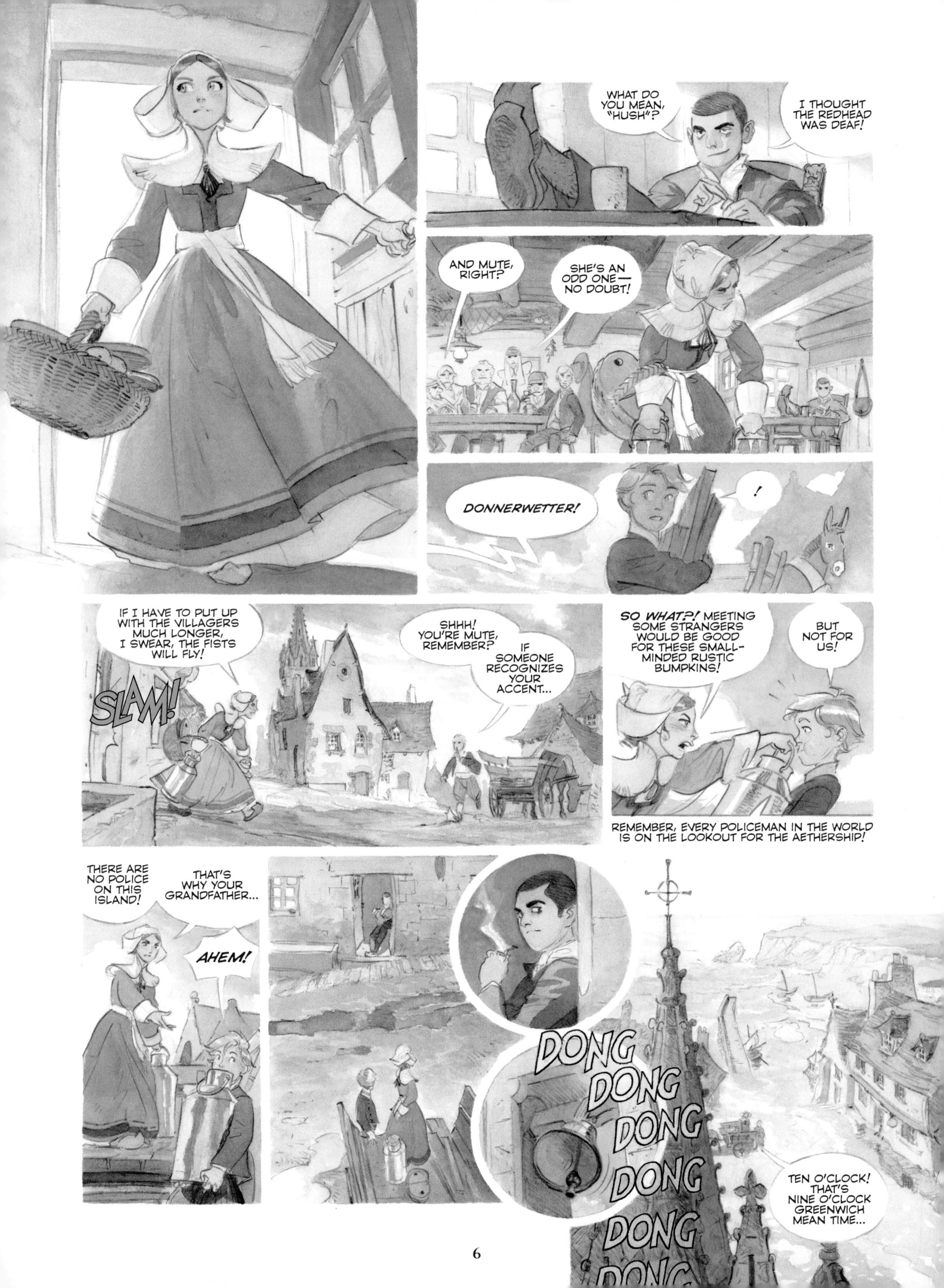
WHAT DO YOU MEAN, "HUSH"?
I THOUGHT THE REDHEAD WAS DEAF!
AND MUTE, RIGHT?
SHE'S AN ODD ONE— NO DOUBT!
DONNERWETTER!
!
IF I HAVE TO PUT UP WITH THE VILLAGERS MUCH LONGER, I SWEAR, THE FISTS WILL FLY!
SLAM!
SHHH! YOU'RE MUTE, REMEMBER?
IF SOMEONE RECOGNIZES YOUR ACCENT...
SO WHAT?! MEETING SOME STRANGERS WOULD BE GOOD FOR THESE SMALL-MINDED RUSTIC BUMPKINS!
BUT NOT FOR US!
REMEMBER, EVERY POLICEMAN IN THE WORLD IS ON THE LOOKOUT FOR THE AETHERSHIP!
THERE ARE NO POLICE ON THIS ISLAND!
THAT'S WHY YOUR GRANDFATHER...
AHEM!
DONG DONG DONG DONG DONG DONG
TEN O'CLOCK! THAT'S NINE O'CLOCK GREENWICH MEAN TIME...

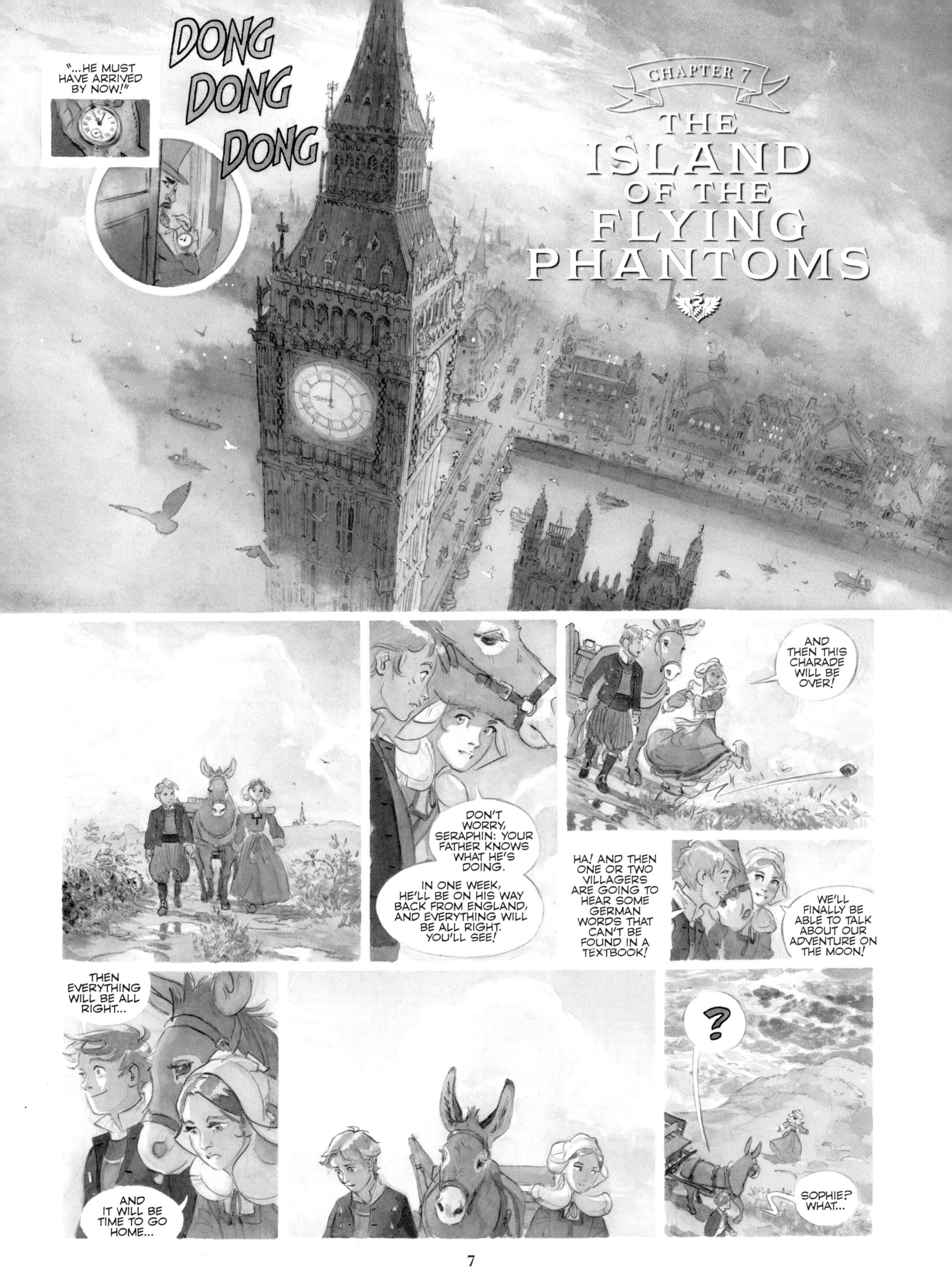
"...HE MUST HAVE ARRIVED BY NOW!"
DONG DONG DONG
CHAPTER 7
THE ISLAND OF THE FLYING PHANTOMS
DON'T WORRY, SERAPHIN: YOUR FATHER KNOWS WHAT HE'S DOING.
IN ONE WEEK, HE'LL BE ON HIS WAY BACK FROM ENGLAND, AND EVERYTHING WILL BE ALL RIGHT. YOU'LL SEE!
AND THEN THIS CHARADE WILL BE OVER!
HA! AND THEN ONE OR TWO VILLAGERS ARE GOING TO HEAR SOME GERMAN WORDS THAT CAN'T BE FOUND IN A TEXTBOOK!
WE'LL FINALLY BE ABLE TO TALK ABOUT OUR ADVENTURE ON THE MOON!
THEN EVERYTHING WILL BE ALL RIGHT...
AND IT WILL BE TIME TO GO HOME...
?
SOPHIE? WHAT...

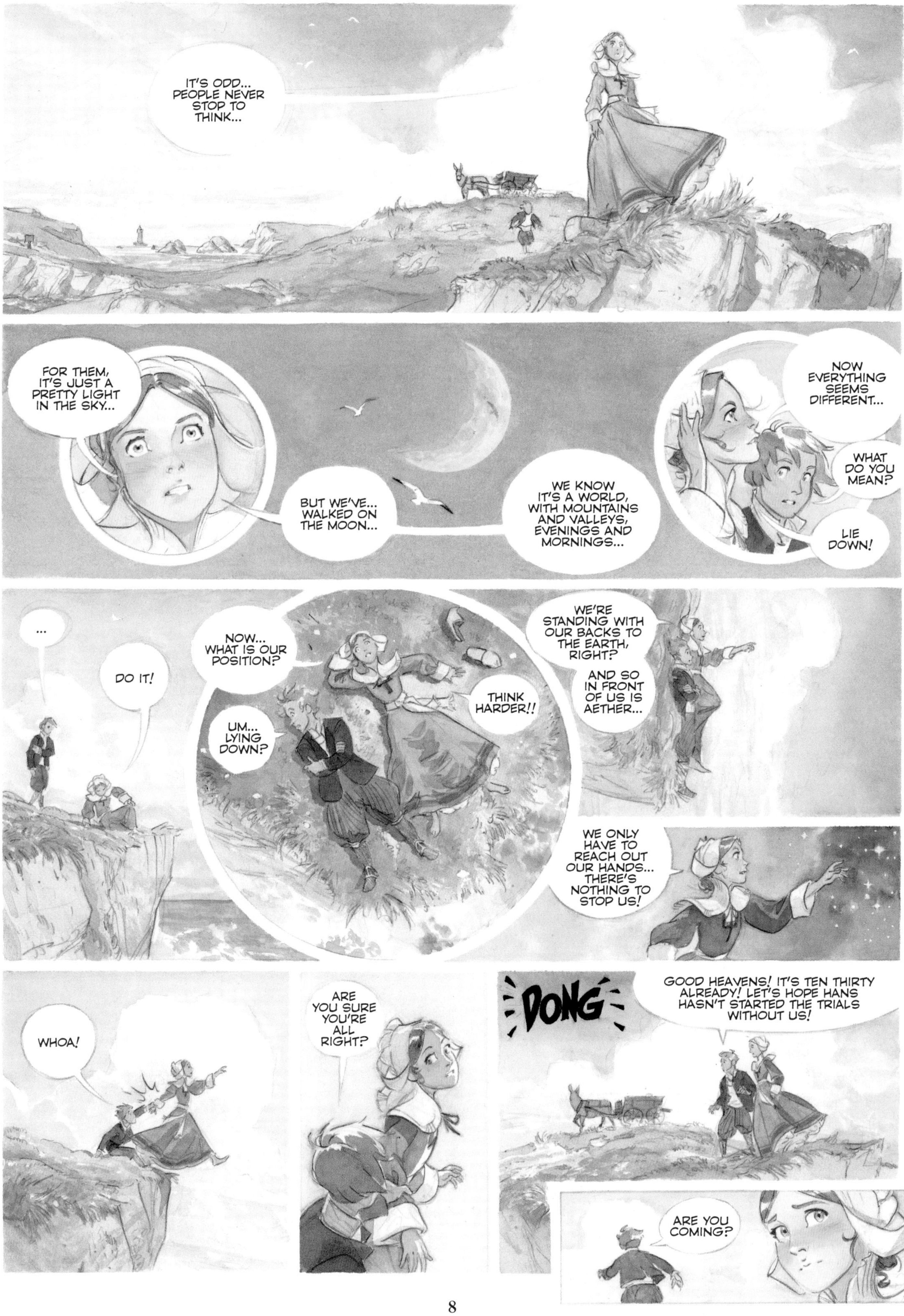

IT'S ODD... PEOPLE NEVER STOP TO THINK...
FOR THEM, IT'S JUST A PRETTY LIGHT IN THE SKY...
BUT WE'VE... WALKED ON THE MOON...
WE KNOW IT'S A WORLD, WITH MOUNTAINS AND VALLEYS, EVENINGS AND MORNINGS...
NOW EVERYTHING SEEMS DIFFERENT...
WHAT DO YOU MEAN?
LIE DOWN!
...
DO IT!
NOW... WHAT IS OUR POSITION?
UM... LYING DOWN?
THINK HARDER!!
WE'RE STANDING WITH OUR BACKS TO THE EARTH, RIGHT?
AND SO IN FRONT OF US IS AETHER...
WE ONLY HAVE TO REACH OUT OUR HANDS... THERE'S NOTHING TO STOP US!
WHOA!
ARE YOU SURE YOU'RE ALL RIGHT?
DONG
GOOD HEAVENS! IT'S TEN THIRTY ALREADY! LET'S HOPE HANS HASN'T STARTED THE TRIALS WITHOUT US!
ARE YOU COMING?

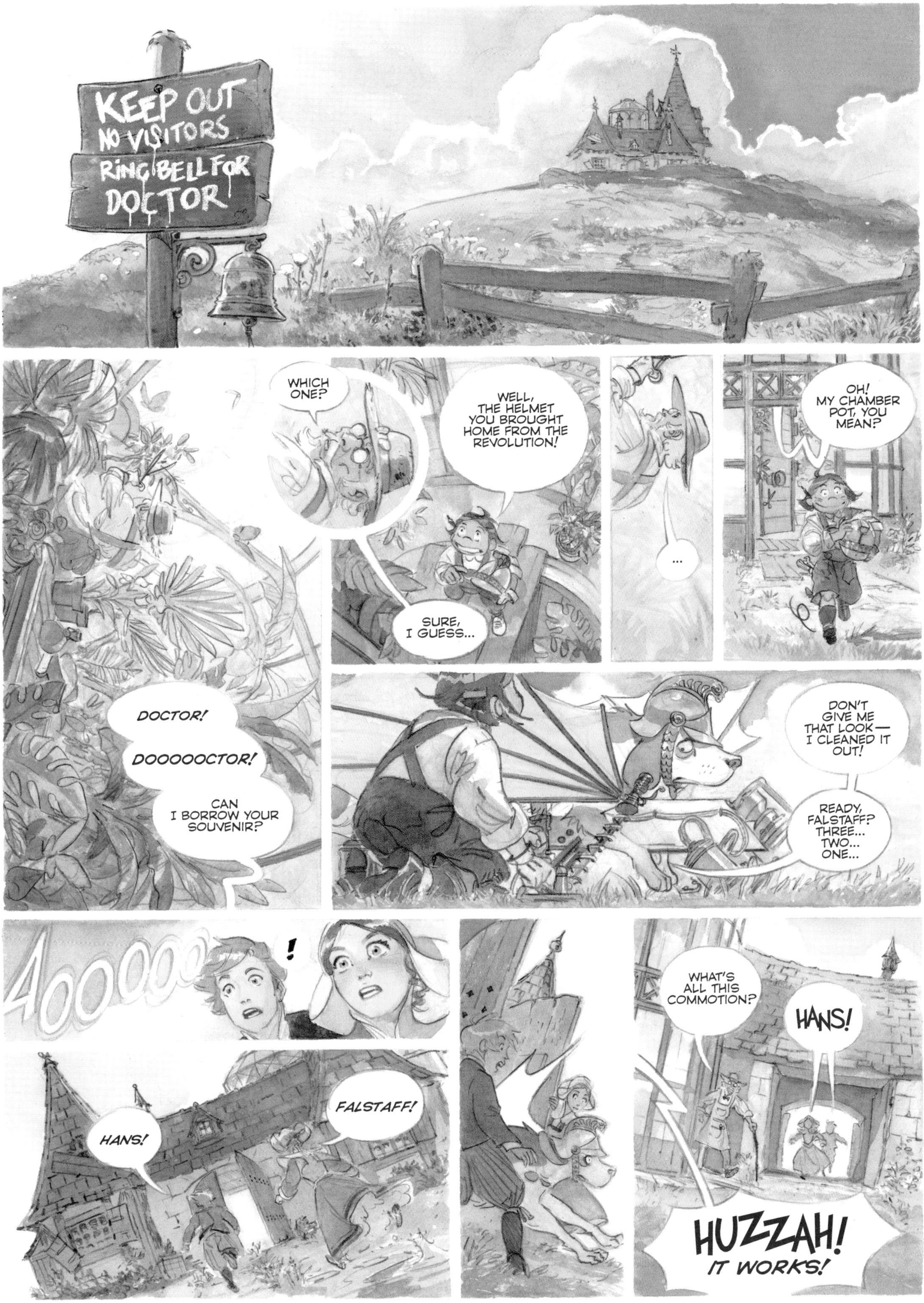
KEEP OUT
NO VISITORS
RING BELL FOR
DOCTOR
DOCTOR!
DOOOOOCTOR!
CAN I BORROW YOUR SOUVENIR?
WHICH ONE?
WELL, THE HELMET YOU BROUGHT HOME FROM THE REVOLUTION!
SURE, I GUESS...
...
OH! MY CHAMBER POT, YOU MEAN?
DON'T GIVE ME THAT LOOK— I CLEANED IT OUT!
READY, FALSTAFF? THREE... TWO... ONE...
400000
!
HANS!
FALSTAFF!
WHAT'S ALL THIS COMMOTION?
HANS!
HUZZAH!
IT WORKS!

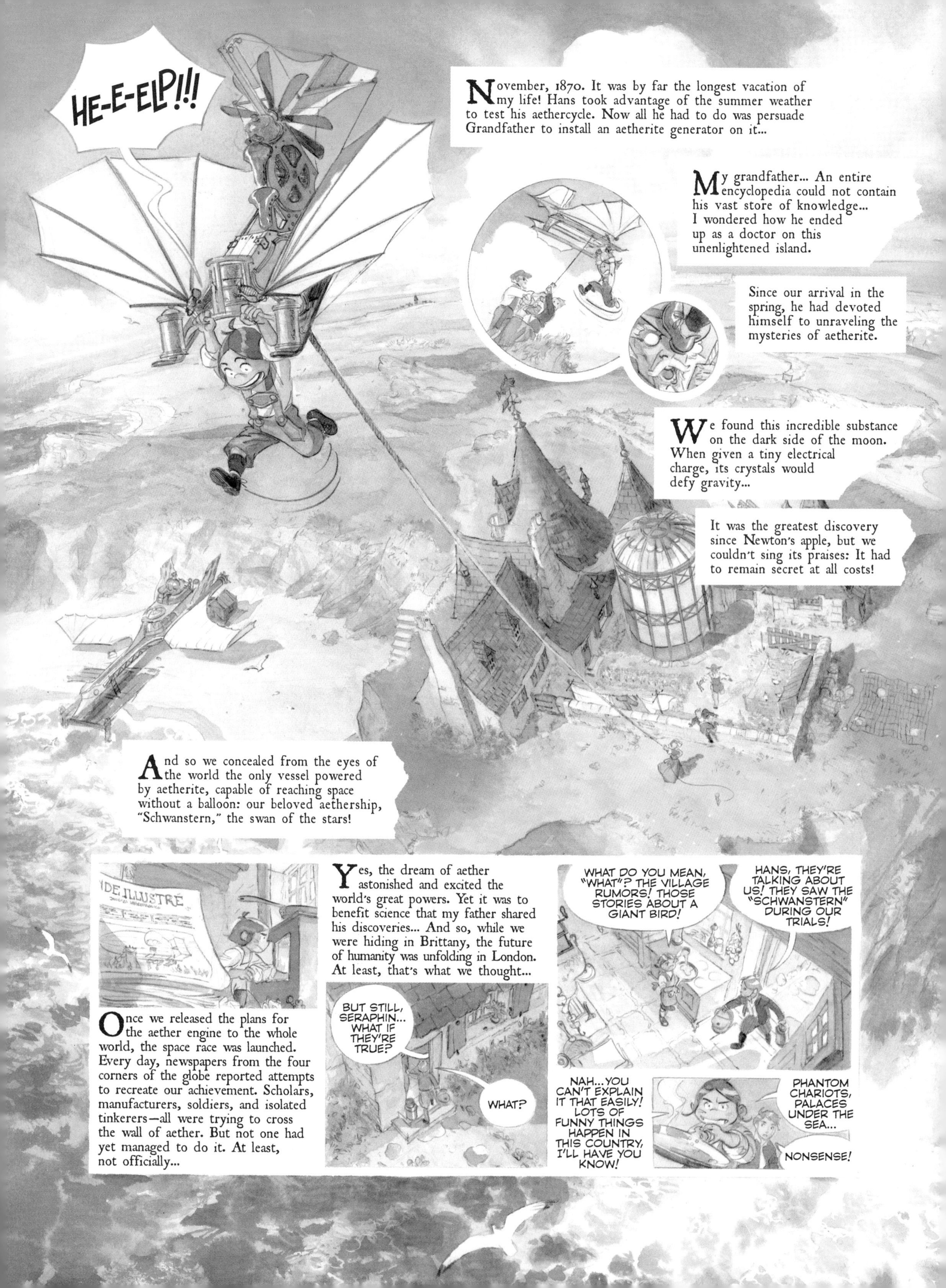
HE-E-ELP!!!
November, 1870. It was by far the longest vacation of my life! Hans took advantage of the summer weather to test his aethercycle. Now all he had to do was persuade Grandfather to install an aetherite generator on it...
My grandfather... An entire encyclopedia could not contain his vast store of knowledge... I wondered how he ended up as a doctor on this unenlightened island.
Since our arrival in the spring, he had devoted himself to unraveling the mysteries of aetherite.
We found this incredible substance on the dark side of the moon. When given a tiny electrical charge, its crystals would defy gravity...
It was the greatest discovery since Newton's apple, but we couldn't sing its praises: It had to remain secret at all costs!
And so we concealed from the eyes of the world the only vessel powered by aetherite, capable of reaching space without a balloon: our beloved aethership, "Schwanstern," the swan of the stars!
Once we released the plans for the aether engine to the whole world, the space race was launched. Every day, newspapers from the four corners of the globe reported attempts to recreate our achievement. Scholars, manufacturers, soldiers, and isolated tinkerers—all were trying to cross the wall of aether. But not one had yet managed to do it. At least, not officially...
Yes, the dream of aether astonished and excited the world's great powers. Yet it was to benefit science that my father shared his discoveries... And so, while we were hiding in Brittany, the future of humanity was unfolding in London. At least, that's what we thought...
BUT STILL, SERAPHIN... WHAT IF THEY'RE TRUE?
WHAT?
WHAT DO YOU MEAN, "WHAT"? THE VILLAGE RUMORS! THOSE STORIES ABOUT A GIANT BIRD!
HANS, THEY'RE TALKING ABOUT US! THEY SAW THE "SCHWANSTERN" DURING OUR TRIALS!
NAH... YOU CAN'T EXPLAIN IT THAT EASILY! LOTS OF FUNNY THINGS HAPPEN IN THIS COUNTRY, I'LL HAVE YOU KNOW!
PHANTOM CHARIOTS, PALACES UNDER THE SEA...
NONSENSE!

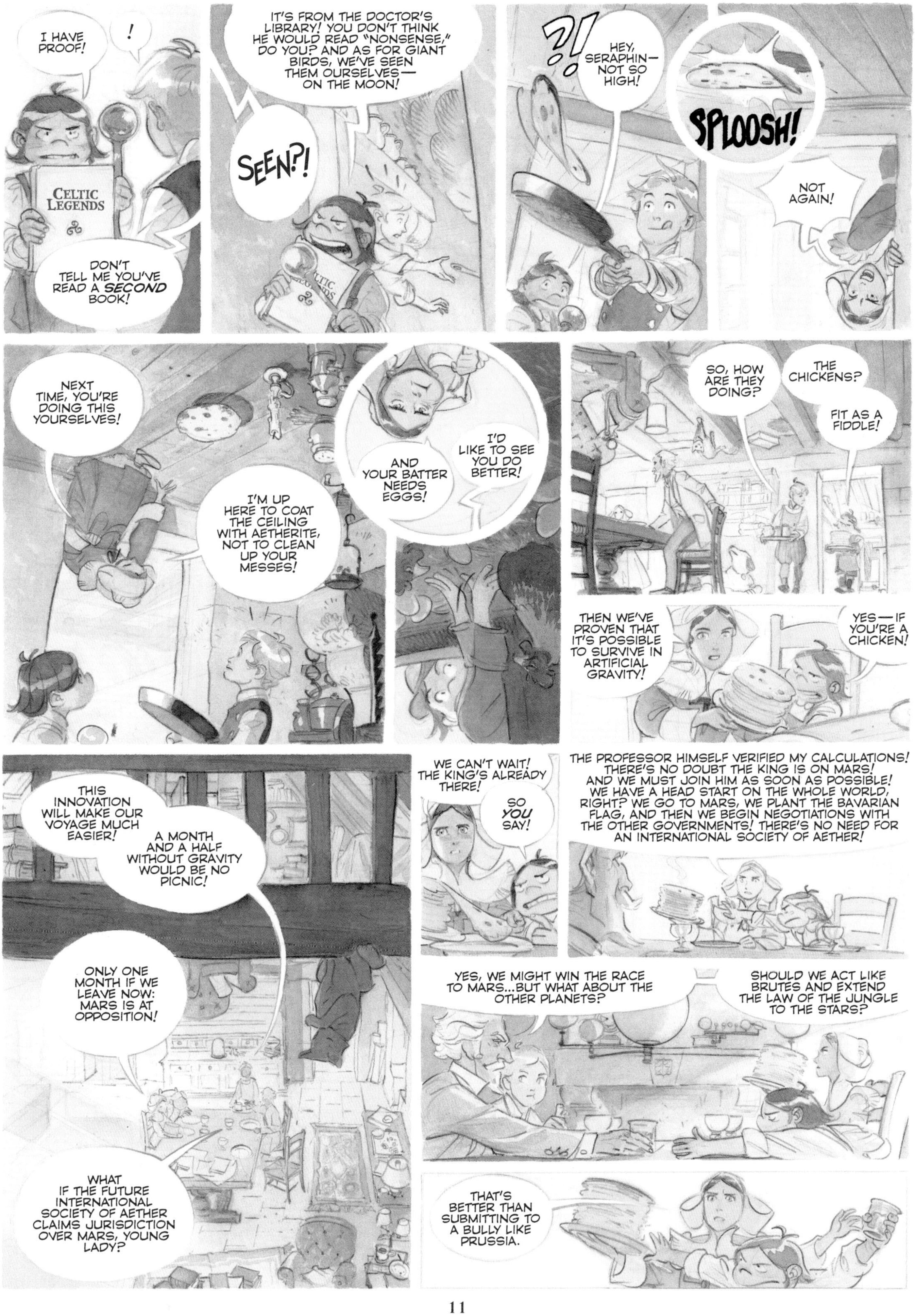
I HAVE PROOF!
!
CELTIC LEGENDS
DON'T TELL ME YOU'VE READ A *SECOND* BOOK!
IT'S FROM THE DOCTOR'S LIBRARY! YOU DON'T THINK HE WOULD READ "NONSENSE," DO YOU? AND AS FOR GIANT BIRDS, WE'VE SEEN THEM OURSELVES—ON THE MOON!
SEEN?!
?!
HEY, SERAPHIN—NOT SO HIGH!
SPLOOSH!
NOT AGAIN!
NEXT TIME, YOU'RE DOING THIS YOURSELVES!
I'M UP HERE TO COAT THE CEILING WITH AETHERITE, NOT TO CLEAN UP YOUR MESSES!
AND YOUR BATTER NEEDS EGGS!
I'D LIKE TO SEE YOU DO BETTER!
SO, HOW ARE THEY DOING?
THE CHICKENS?
FIT AS A FIDDLE!
THEN WE'VE PROVEN THAT IT'S POSSIBLE TO SURVIVE IN ARTIFICIAL GRAVITY!
YES—IF YOU'RE A CHICKEN!
THIS INNOVATION WILL MAKE OUR VOYAGE MUCH EASIER!
A MONTH AND A HALF WITHOUT GRAVITY WOULD BE NO PICNIC!
ONLY ONE MONTH IF WE LEAVE NOW: MARS IS AT OPPOSITION!
WHAT IF THE FUTURE INTERNATIONAL SOCIETY OF AETHER CLAIMS JURISDICTION OVER MARS, YOUNG LADY?
WE CAN'T WAIT! THE KING'S ALREADY THERE!
SO *YOU* SAY!
THE PROFESSOR HIMSELF VERIFIED MY CALCULATIONS! THERE'S NO DOUBT THE KING IS ON MARS! AND WE MUST JOIN HIM AS SOON AS POSSIBLE! WE HAVE A HEAD START ON THE WHOLE WORLD, RIGHT? WE GO TO MARS, WE PLANT THE BAVARIAN FLAG, AND THEN WE BEGIN NEGOTIATIONS WITH THE OTHER GOVERNMENTS! THERE'S NO NEED FOR AN INTERNATIONAL SOCIETY OF AETHER!
YES, WE MIGHT WIN THE RACE TO MARS...BUT WHAT ABOUT THE OTHER PLANETS?
SHOULD WE ACT LIKE BRUTES AND EXTEND THE LAW OF THE JUNGLE TO THE STARS?
THAT'S BETTER THAN SUBMITTING TO A BULLY LIKE PRUSSIA.

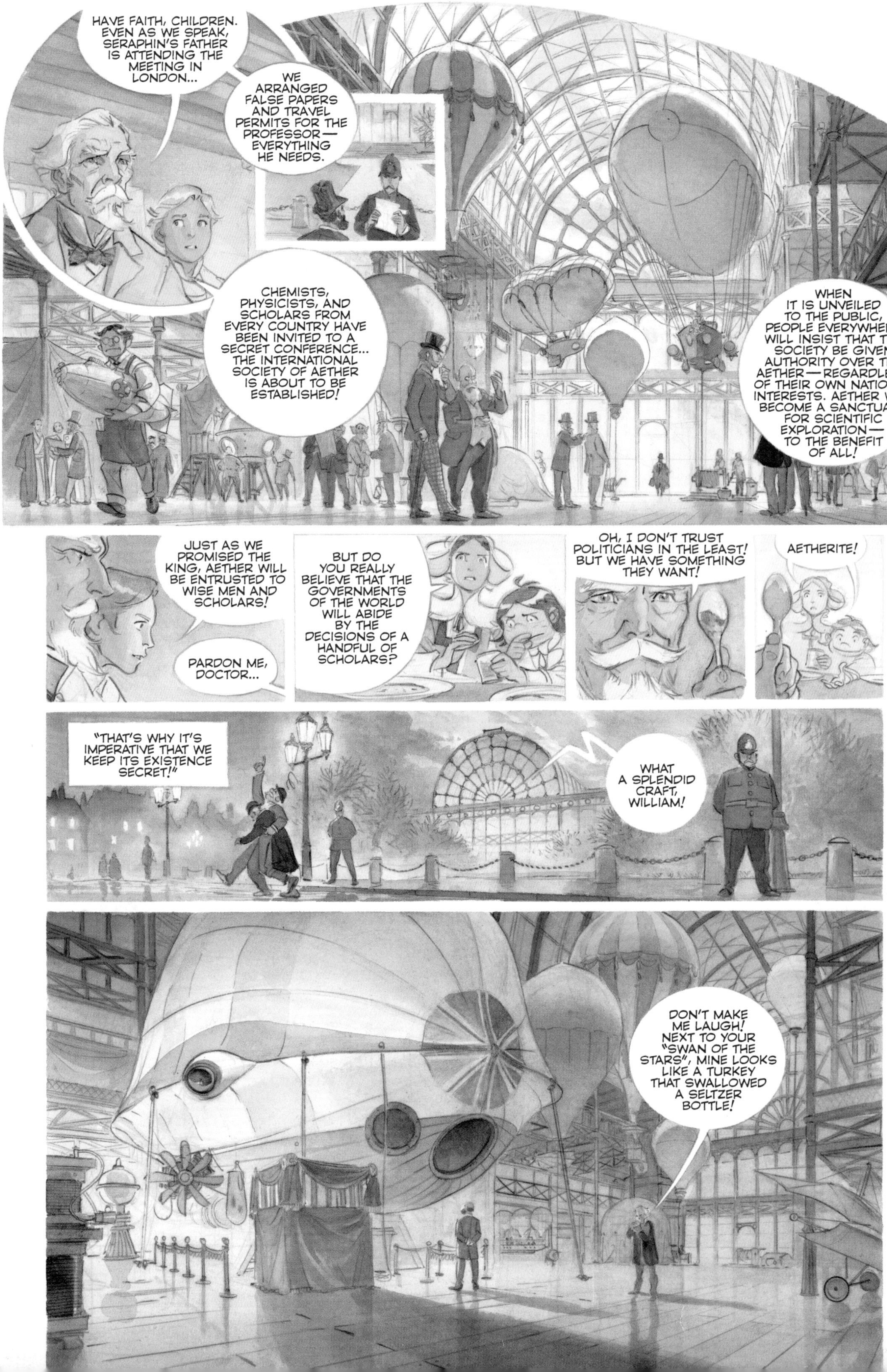
HAVE FAITH, CHILDREN. EVEN AS WE SPEAK, SERAPHIN'S FATHER IS ATTENDING THE MEETING IN LONDON...
WE ARRANGED FALSE PAPERS AND TRAVEL PERMITS FOR THE PROFESSOR— EVERYTHING HE NEEDS.
CHEMISTS, PHYSICISTS, AND SCHOLARS FROM EVERY COUNTRY HAVE BEEN INVITED TO A SECRET CONFERENCE... THE INTERNATIONAL SOCIETY OF AETHER IS ABOUT TO BE ESTABLISHED!
WHEN IT IS UNVEILED TO THE PUBLIC, PEOPLE EVERYWHERE WILL INSIST THAT THE SOCIETY BE GIVEN AUTHORITY OVER THE AETHER—REGARDLESS OF THEIR OWN NATIONAL INTERESTS. AETHER WILL BECOME A SANCTUARY FOR SCIENTIFIC EXPLORATION— TO THE BENEFIT OF ALL!
JUST AS WE PROMISED THE KING, AETHER WILL BE ENTRUSTED TO WISE MEN AND SCHOLARS!
PARDON ME, DOCTOR...
BUT DO YOU REALLY BELIEVE THAT THE GOVERNMENTS OF THE WORLD WILL ABIDE BY THE DECISIONS OF A HANDFUL OF SCHOLARS?
OH, I DON'T TRUST POLITICIANS IN THE LEAST! BUT WE HAVE SOMETHING THEY WANT!
AETHERITE!
"THAT'S WHY IT'S IMPERATIVE THAT WE KEEP ITS EXISTENCE SECRET!"
WHAT A SPLENDID CRAFT, WILLIAM!
DON'T MAKE ME LAUGH! NEXT TO YOUR "SWAN OF THE STARS", MINE LOOKS LIKE A TURKEY THAT SWALLOWED A SELTZER BOTTLE!

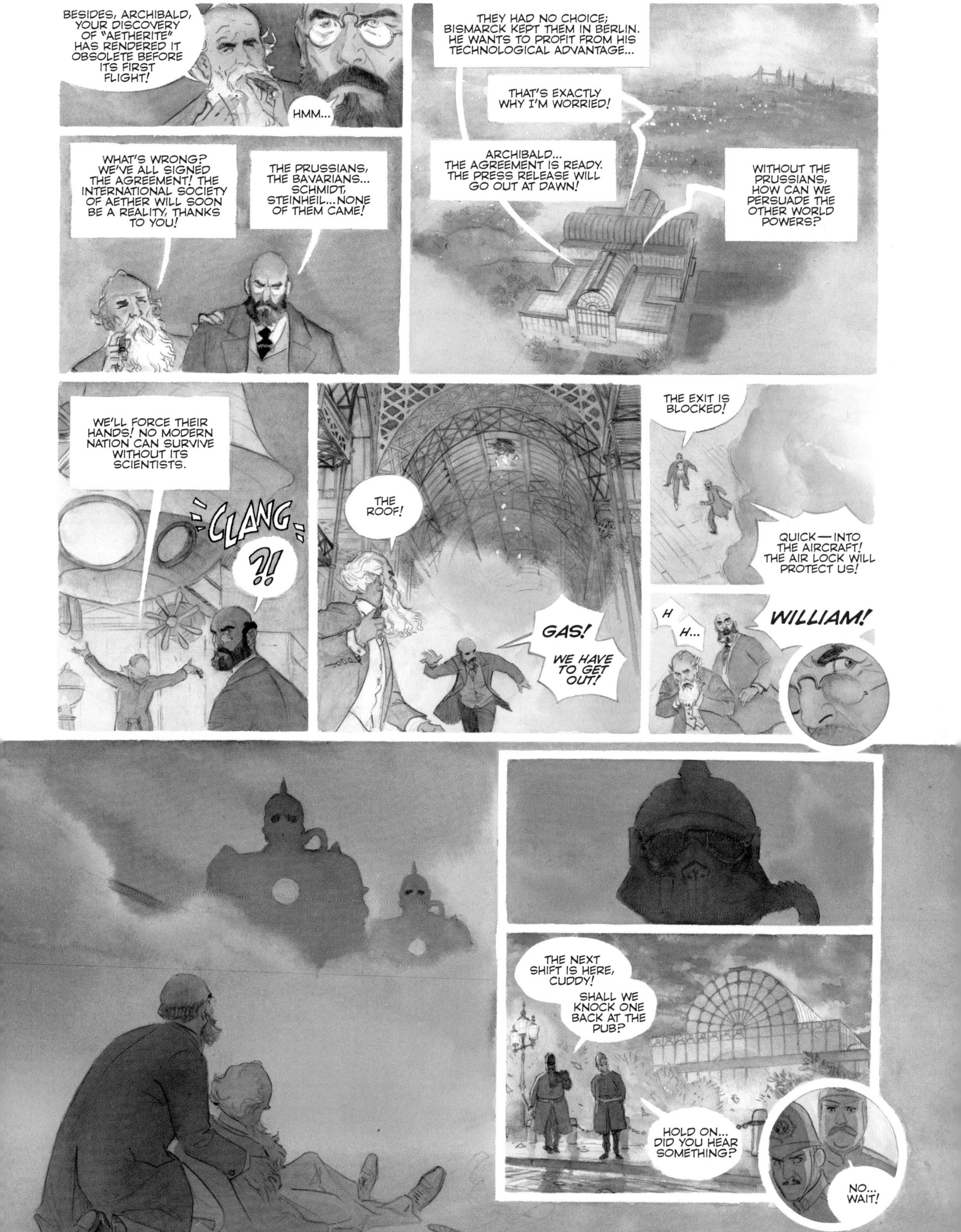
BESIDES, ARCHIBALD, YOUR DISCOVERY OF "AETHERITE" HAS RENDERED IT OBSOLETE BEFORE ITS FIRST FLIGHT!
HMM...
WHAT'S WRONG? WE'VE ALL SIGNED THE AGREEMENT! THE INTERNATIONAL SOCIETY OF AETHER WILL SOON BE A REALITY, THANKS TO YOU!
THE PRUSSIANS, THE BAVARIANS... SCHMIDT, STEINHEIL... NONE OF THEM CAME!
THEY HAD NO CHOICE; BISMARCK KEPT THEM IN BERLIN. HE WANTS TO PROFIT FROM HIS TECHNOLOGICAL ADVANTAGE...
THAT'S EXACTLY WHY I'M WORRIED!
ARCHIBALD... THE AGREEMENT IS READY. THE PRESS RELEASE WILL GO OUT AT DAWN!
WITHOUT THE PRUSSIANS, HOW CAN WE PERSUADE THE OTHER WORLD POWERS?
WE'LL FORCE THEIR HANDS! NO MODERN NATION CAN SURVIVE WITHOUT ITS SCIENTISTS.
CLANG
?!
THE ROOF!
GAS!
WE HAVE TO GET OUT!
THE EXIT IS BLOCKED!
QUICK — INTO THE AIRCRAFT! THE AIR LOCK WILL PROTECT US!
H
H...
WILLIAM!
THE NEXT SHIFT IS HERE, CUDDY!
SHALL WE KNOCK ONE BACK AT THE PUB?
HOLD ON... DID YOU HEAR SOMETHING?
NO... WAIT!

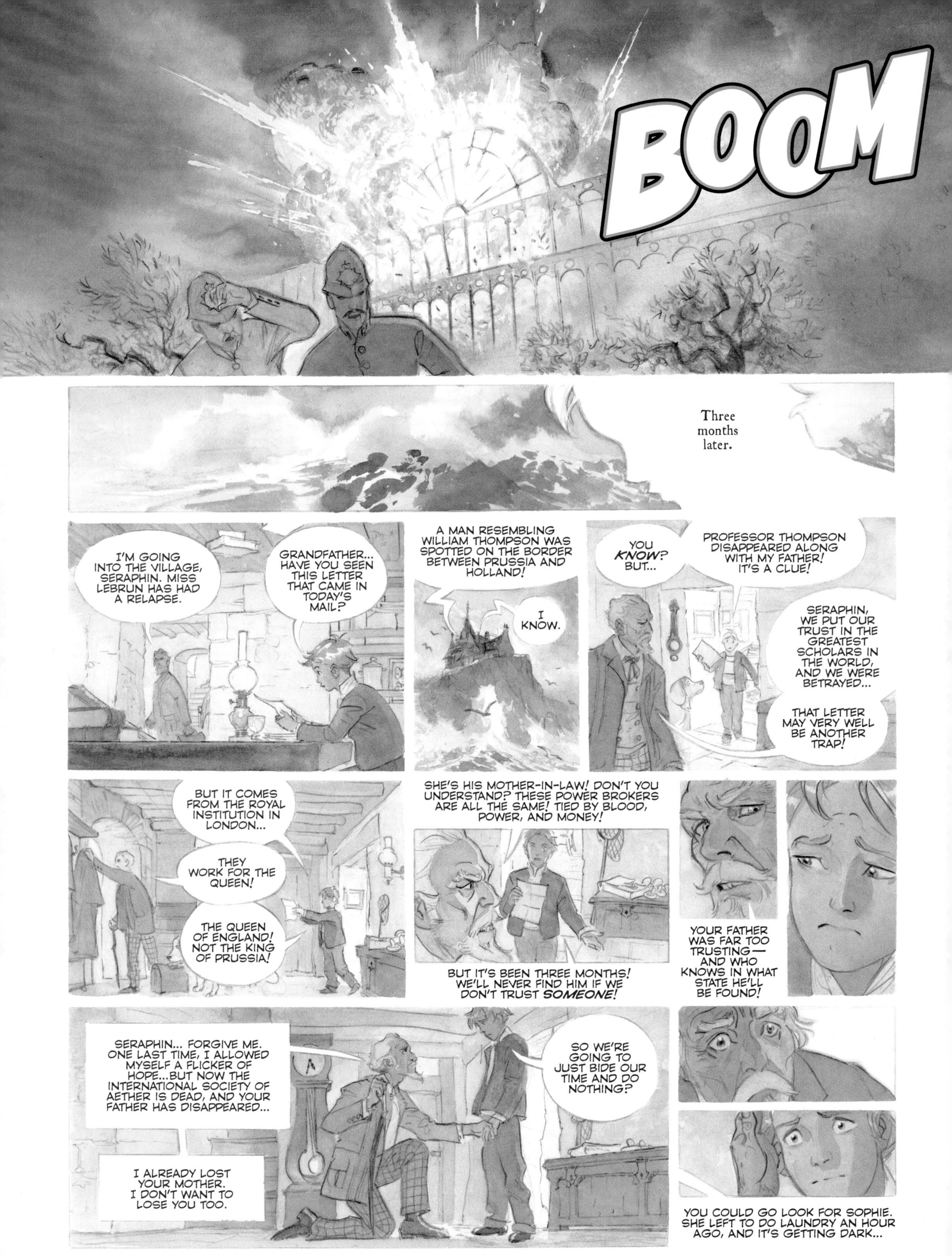
BOOM
Three months later.
I'M GOING INTO THE VILLAGE, SERAPHIN. MISS LEBRUN HAS HAD A RELAPSE.
GRANDFATHER... HAVE YOU SEEN THIS LETTER THAT CAME IN TODAY'S MAIL?
A MAN RESEMBLING WILLIAM THOMPSON WAS SPOTTED ON THE BORDER BETWEEN PRUSSIA AND HOLLAND!
I KNOW.
YOU KNOW? BUT...
PROFESSOR THOMPSON DISAPPEARED ALONG WITH MY FATHER! IT'S A CLUE!
SERAPHIN, WE PUT OUR TRUST IN THE GREATEST SCHOLARS IN THE WORLD, AND WE WERE BETRAYED...
THAT LETTER MAY VERY WELL BE ANOTHER TRAP!
BUT IT COMES FROM THE ROYAL INSTITUTION IN LONDON...
THEY WORK FOR THE QUEEN!
THE QUEEN OF ENGLAND! NOT THE KING OF PRUSSIA!
SHE'S HIS MOTHER-IN-LAW! DON'T YOU UNDERSTAND? THESE POWER BROKERS ARE ALL THE SAME! TIED BY BLOOD, POWER, AND MONEY!
BUT IT'S BEEN THREE MONTHS! WE'LL NEVER FIND HIM IF WE DON'T TRUST SOMEONE!
YOUR FATHER WAS FAR TOO TRUSTING—AND WHO KNOWS IN WHAT STATE HE'LL BE FOUND!
SERAPHIN... FORGIVE ME. ONE LAST TIME, I ALLOWED MYSELF A FLICKER OF HOPE...BUT NOW THE INTERNATIONAL SOCIETY OF AETHER IS DEAD, AND YOUR FATHER HAS DISAPPEARED...
I ALREADY LOST YOUR MOTHER. I DON'T WANT TO LOSE YOU TOO.
SO WE'RE GOING TO JUST BIDE OUR TIME AND DO NOTHING?
YOU COULD GO LOOK FOR SOPHIE. SHE LEFT TO DO LAUNDRY AN HOUR AGO, AND IT'S GETTING DARK...

ONCE AGAIN STORIES OF A GIANT BIRD ARE SWEEPING THE VILLAGE. PLUS, A LIGHTHOUSE KEEPER HAS GONE MISSING... I'VE NO DOUBT HE'LL AWAKEN IN SOME COVE WITH QUITE A HANGOVER... BUT FOR NOW, IN THE VILLAGE, NO ONE WILL EVEN GREET ME.

BUT WE KNOW HOW THESE STORIES START! WHAT ARE YOU AFRAID OF?

FEAR ITSELF.

GO FIND SOPHIE, WILL YOU? HANS WILL KEEP WATCH OVER THE HOUSE.

ARE YOU GOING OUT?

MAKE SURE YOU'RE BACK BEFORE NIGHTFALL...

AND BEWARE THE ANKOU!

I had spent several vacations at my grandfather's house. I knew all about the water spirits, who live under the sea in their submerged villages...

...and the Treo-Fall, goblins who cause vertigo to those at the edge of high cliffs...

I didn't believe in them, of course, but that didn't stop me from listening for the mournful groaning sound...

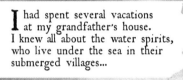

...of the ghostly cart drawn by Ankou, the Servant of Death...

...whose arrival announces the passing of a loved one.

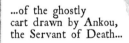

For my father was never far from my thoughts.

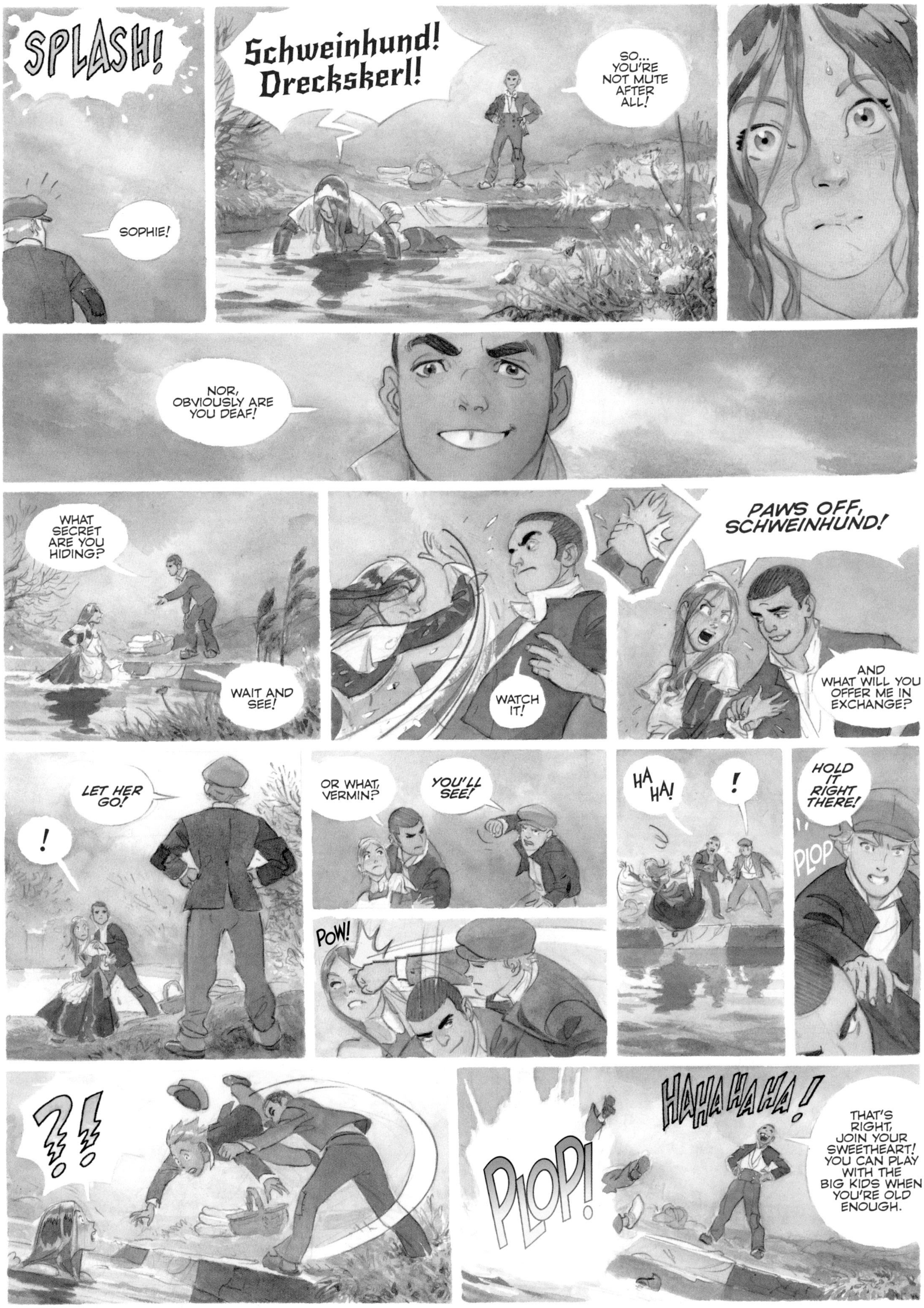
SPLASH!
SOPHIE!
Schweinhund! Dreckskerl!
SO... YOU'RE NOT MUTE AFTER ALL!
NOR, OBVIOUSLY ARE YOU DEAF!
WHAT SECRET ARE YOU HIDING?
WAIT AND SEE!
WATCH IT!
PAWS OFF, SCHWEINHUND!
AND WHAT WILL YOU OFFER ME IN EXCHANGE?
LET HER GO!
!
OR WHAT, VERMIN?
YOU'LL SEE!
POW!
HA HA!
!
HOLD IT RIGHT THERE!
PLOP
?!
HAHAHAHA!
PLOP!
THAT'S RIGHT, JOIN YOUR SWEETHEART! YOU CAN PLAY WITH THE BIG KIDS WHEN YOU'RE OLD ENOUGH.

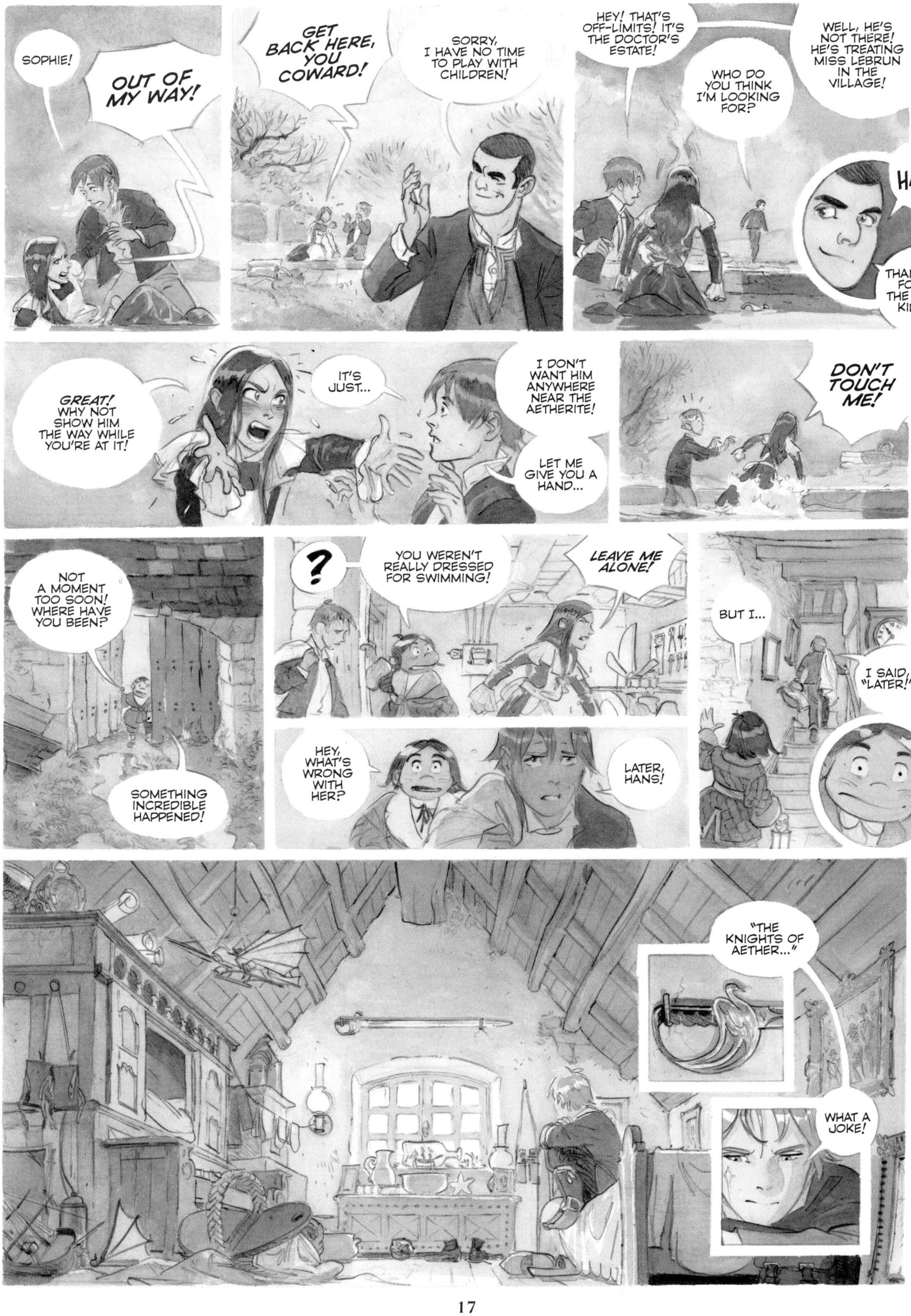
SOPHIE!
OUT OF MY WAY!
GET BACK HERE, YOU COWARD!
SORRY, I HAVE NO TIME TO PLAY WITH CHILDREN!
HEY! THAT'S OFF-LIMITS! IT'S THE DOCTOR'S ESTATE!
WHO DO YOU THINK I'M LOOKING FOR?
WELL, HE'S NOT THERE! HE'S TREATING MISS LEBRUN IN THE VILLAGE!
HA!
THANKS FOR THE TIP, KID!
GREAT! WHY NOT SHOW HIM THE WAY WHILE YOU'RE AT IT!
IT'S JUST...
I DON'T WANT HIM ANYWHERE NEAR THE AETHERITE!
LET ME GIVE YOU A HAND...
DON'T TOUCH ME!
NOT A MOMENT TOO SOON! WHERE HAVE YOU BEEN?
SOMETHING INCREDIBLE HAPPENED!
?
YOU WEREN'T REALLY DRESSED FOR SWIMMING!
LEAVE ME ALONE!
HEY, WHAT'S WRONG WITH HER?
LATER, HANS!
BUT I...
I SAID, "LATER!"
"THE KNIGHTS OF AETHER..."
WHAT A JOKE!

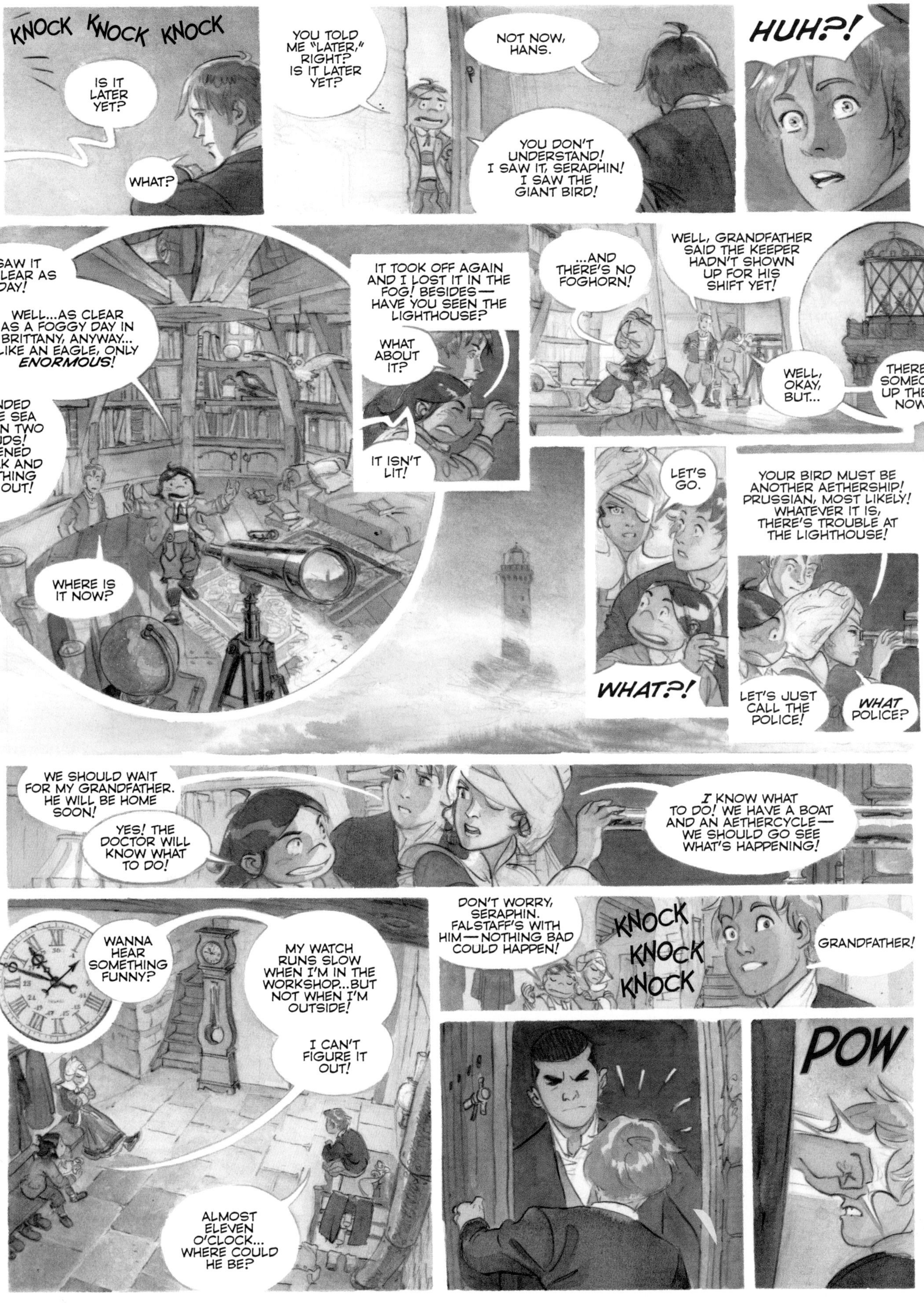
KNOCK KNOCK KNOCK
IS IT LATER YET?
WHAT?
YOU TOLD ME "LATER," RIGHT? IS IT LATER YET?
NOT NOW, HANS.
YOU DON'T UNDERSTAND! I SAW IT, SERAPHIN! I SAW THE GIANT BIRD!
HUH?!
I SAW IT AS CLEAR AS DAY!
WELL...AS CLEAR AS A FOGGY DAY IN BRITTANY, ANYWAY... LIKE AN EAGLE, ONLY *ENORMOUS*!
IT LANDED ON THE SEA BETWEEN TWO CLOUDS! IT OPENED ITS BEAK AND SOMETHING CAME OUT!
WHERE IS IT NOW?
IT TOOK OFF AGAIN AND I LOST IT IN THE FOG! BESIDES— HAVE YOU SEEN THE LIGHTHOUSE?
WHAT ABOUT IT?
IT ISN'T LIT!
...AND THERE'S NO FOGHORN!
WELL, GRANDFATHER SAID THE KEEPER HADN'T SHOWN UP FOR HIS SHIFT YET!
WELL, OKAY, BUT...
THERE'S SOMEONE UP THERE NOW!
LET'S GO.
WHAT?!
YOUR BIRD MUST BE ANOTHER AETHERSHIP! PRUSSIAN, MOST LIKELY! WHATEVER IT IS, THERE'S TROUBLE AT THE LIGHTHOUSE!
LET'S JUST CALL THE POLICE!
*WHAT* POLICE?
WE SHOULD WAIT FOR MY GRANDFATHER. HE WILL BE HOME SOON!
YES! THE DOCTOR WILL KNOW WHAT TO DO!
*I* KNOW WHAT TO DO! WE HAVE A BOAT AND AN AETHERCYCLE— WE SHOULD GO SEE WHAT'S HAPPENING!
WANNA HEAR SOMETHING FUNNY?
MY WATCH RUNS SLOW WHEN I'M IN THE WORKSHOP...BUT NOT WHEN I'M OUTSIDE!
I CAN'T FIGURE IT OUT!
ALMOST ELEVEN O'CLOCK... WHERE COULD HE BE?
DON'T WORRY, SERAPHIN. FALSTAFF'S WITH HIM—NOTHING BAD COULD HAPPEN!
KNOCK KNOCK KNOCK
GRANDFATHER!
POW

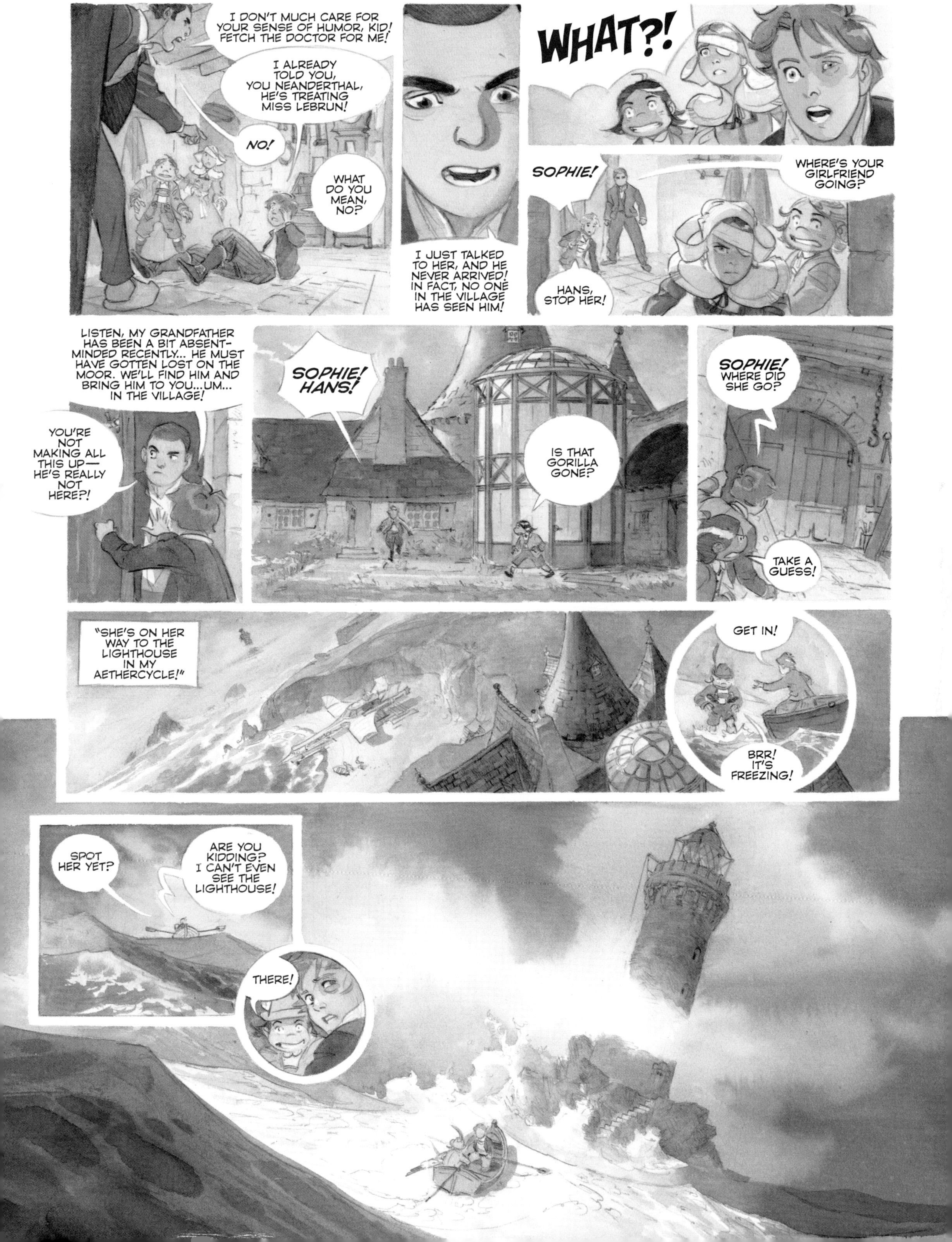

I DON'T MUCH CARE FOR YOUR SENSE OF HUMOR, KID! FETCH THE DOCTOR FOR ME!
I ALREADY TOLD YOU, YOU NEANDERTHAL, HE'S TREATING MISS LEBRUN!
NO!
WHAT DO YOU MEAN, NO?
I JUST TALKED TO HER, AND HE NEVER ARRIVED! IN FACT, NO ONE IN THE VILLAGE HAS SEEN HIM!
WHAT?!
SOPHIE!
WHERE'S YOUR GIRLFRIEND GOING?
HANS, STOP HER!
LISTEN, MY GRANDFATHER HAS BEEN A BIT ABSENT-MINDED RECENTLY... HE MUST HAVE GOTTEN LOST ON THE MOOR. WE'LL FIND HIM AND BRING HIM TO YOU...UM... IN THE VILLAGE!
YOU'RE NOT MAKING ALL THIS UP—HE'S REALLY NOT HERE?!
SOPHIE! HANS!
IS THAT GORILLA GONE?
SOPHIE! WHERE DID SHE GO?
TAKE A GUESS!
"SHE'S ON HER WAY TO THE LIGHTHOUSE IN MY AETHERCYCLE!"
GET IN!
BRR! IT'S FREEZING!
SPOT HER YET?
ARE YOU KIDDING? I CAN'T EVEN SEE THE LIGHTHOUSE!
THERE!

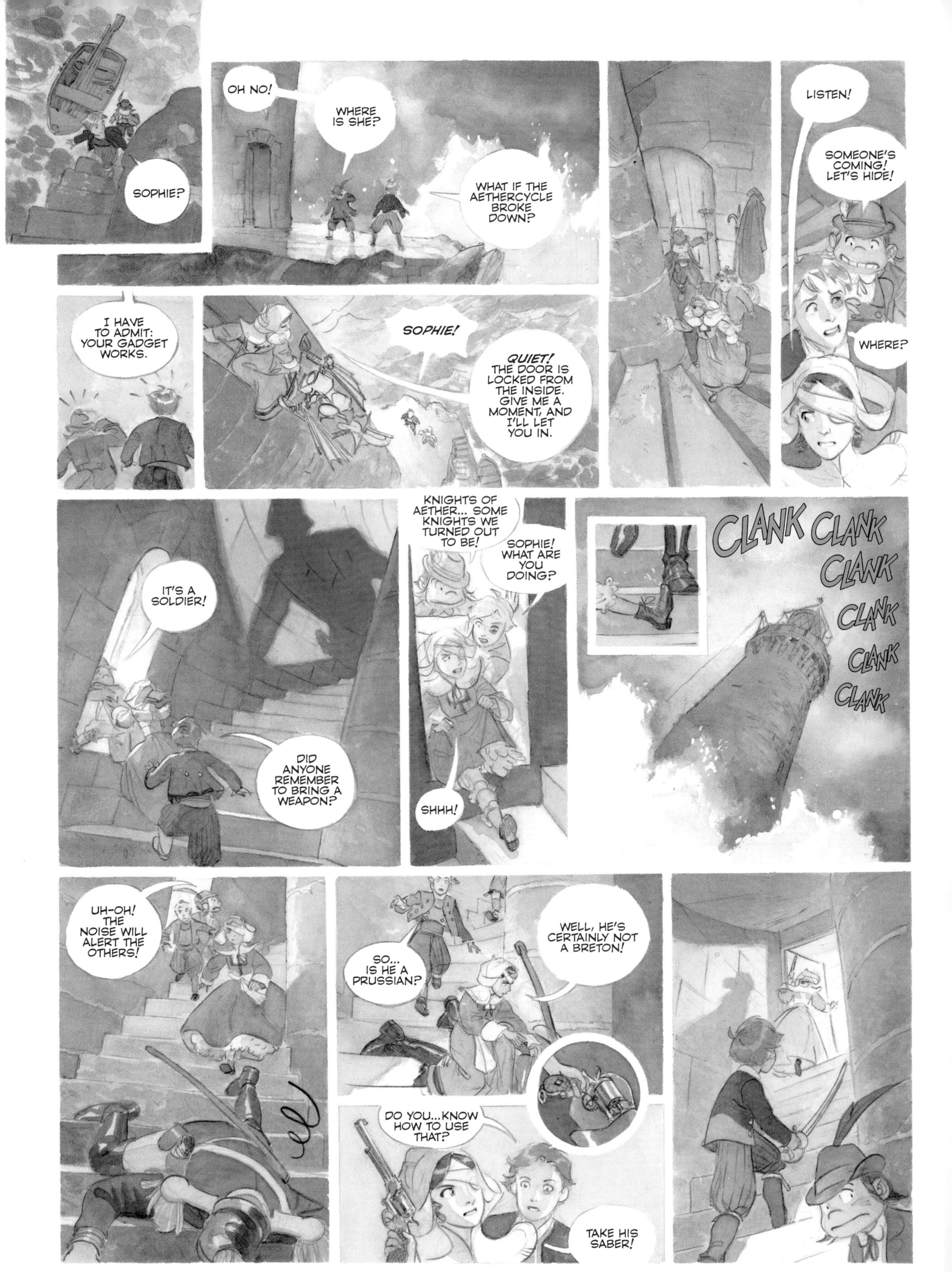
SOPHIE?
OH NO!
WHERE IS SHE?
WHAT IF THE AETHERCYCLE BROKE DOWN?
LISTEN!
SOMEONE'S COMING! LET'S HIDE!
WHERE?
I HAVE TO ADMIT: YOUR GADGET WORKS.
SOPHIE!
QUIET! THE DOOR IS LOCKED FROM THE INSIDE. GIVE ME A MOMENT, AND I'LL LET YOU IN.
IT'S A SOLDIER!
DID ANYONE REMEMBER TO BRING A WEAPON?
KNIGHTS OF AETHER... SOME KNIGHTS WE TURNED OUT TO BE!
SOPHIE! WHAT ARE YOU DOING?
SHHH!
CLANK CLANK CLANK CLANK CLANK CLANK
UH-OH! THE NOISE WILL ALERT THE OTHERS!
SO... IS HE A PRUSSIAN?
WELL, HE'S CERTAINLY NOT A BRETON!
DO YOU...KNOW HOW TO USE THAT?
TAKE HIS SABER!

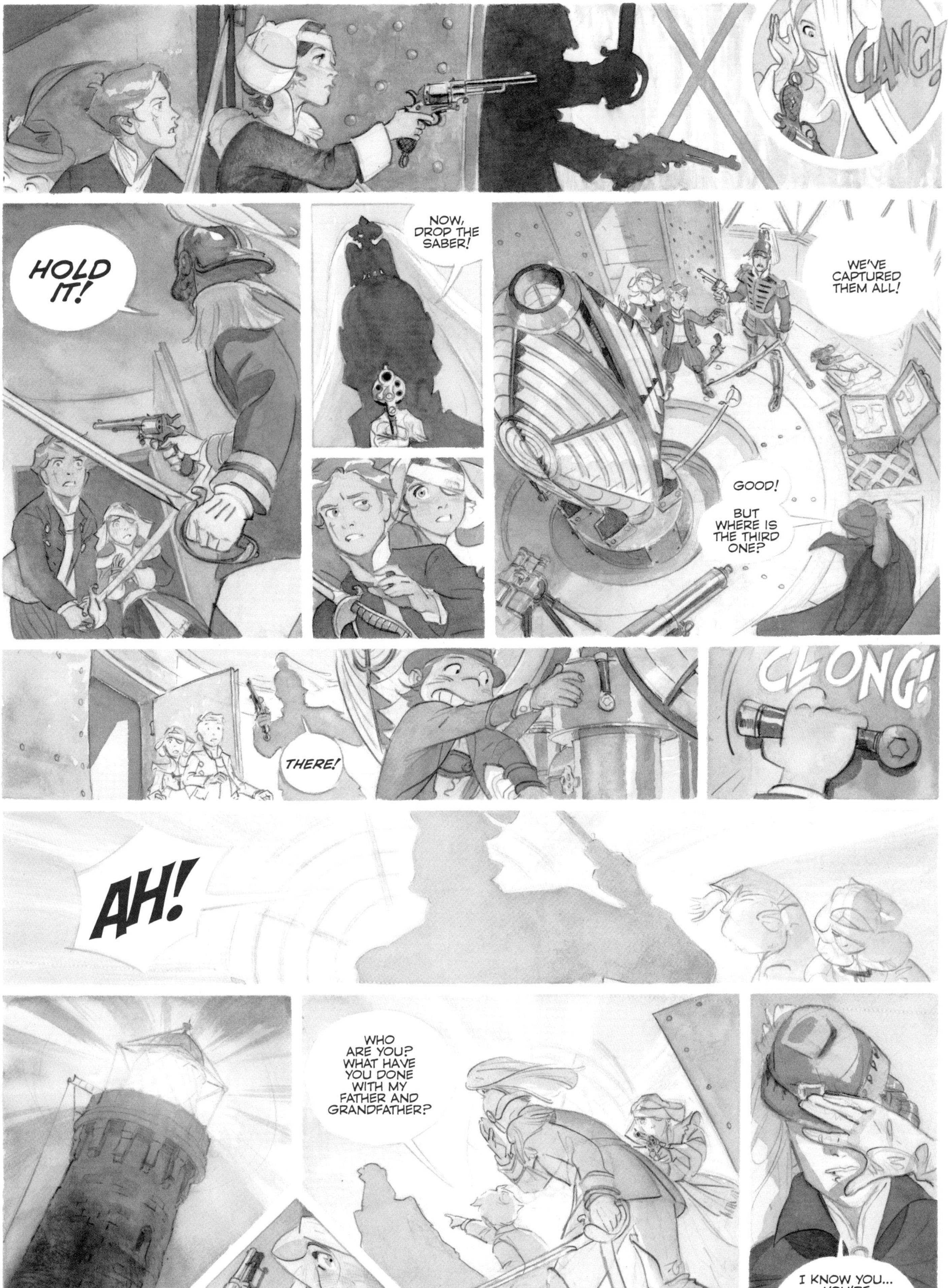
CLANG!
HOLD IT!
NOW, DROP THE SABER!
WE'VE CAPTURED THEM ALL!
GOOD!
BUT WHERE IS THE THIRD ONE?
THERE!
CLONG!
AH!
WHO ARE YOU? WHAT HAVE YOU DONE WITH MY FATHER AND GRANDFATHER?
I KNOW YOU... YOU'RE SERAPHIN DULAC, AREN'T YOU?

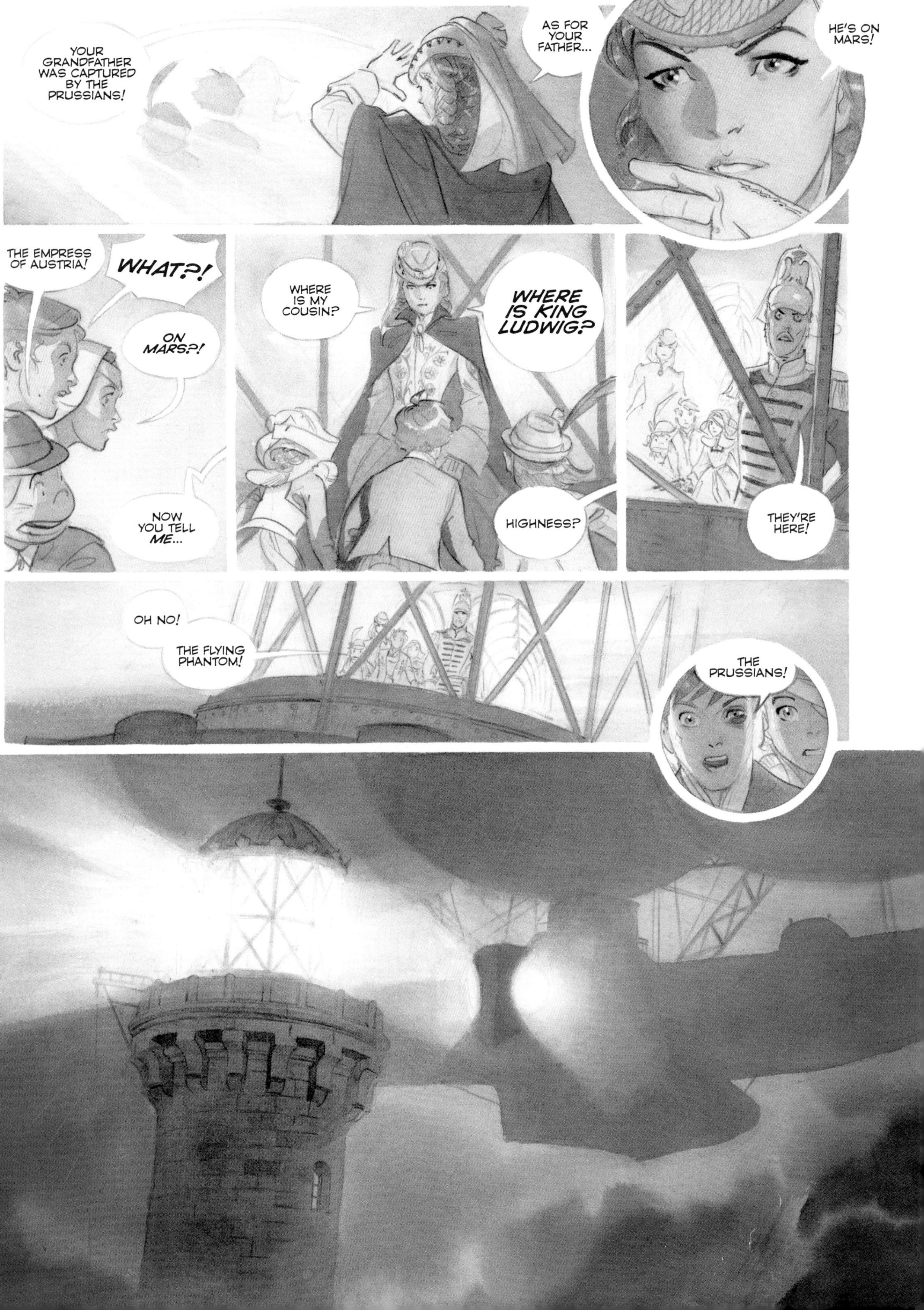
YOUR GRANDFATHER WAS CAPTURED BY THE PRUSSIANS!
AS FOR YOUR FATHER...
HE'S ON MARS!
THE EMPRESS OF AUSTRIA!
WHAT?!
ON MARS?!
NOW YOU TELL ME...
WHERE IS MY COUSIN?
WHERE IS KING LUDWIG?
HIGHNESS?
THEY'RE HERE!
OH NO!
THE FLYING PHANTOM!
THE PRUSSIANS!

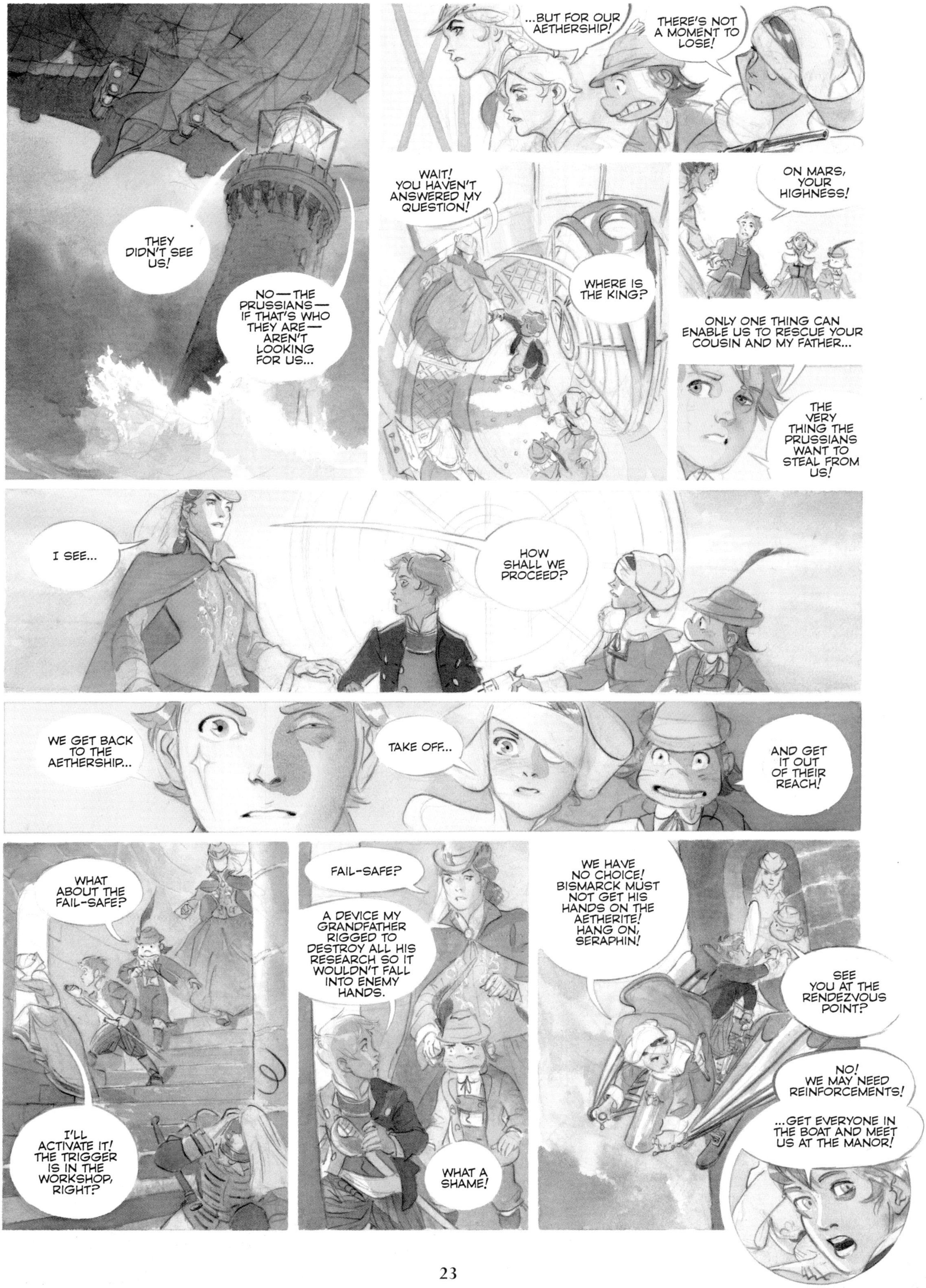
THEY DIDN'T SEE US!
NO—THE PRUSSIANS—IF THAT'S WHO THEY ARE—AREN'T LOOKING FOR US...
...BUT FOR OUR AETHERSHIP!
THERE'S NOT A MOMENT TO LOSE!
WAIT! YOU HAVEN'T ANSWERED MY QUESTION!
WHERE IS THE KING?
ON MARS, YOUR HIGHNESS!
ONLY ONE THING CAN ENABLE US TO RESCUE YOUR COUSIN AND MY FATHER...
THE VERY THING THE PRUSSIANS WANT TO STEAL FROM US!
I SEE...
HOW SHALL WE PROCEED?
WE GET BACK TO THE AETHERSHIP...
TAKE OFF...
AND GET IT OUT OF THEIR REACH!
WHAT ABOUT THE FAIL-SAFE?
I'LL ACTIVATE IT! THE TRIGGER IS IN THE WORKSHOP, RIGHT?
FAIL-SAFE?
A DEVICE MY GRANDFATHER RIGGED TO DESTROY ALL HIS RESEARCH SO IT WOULDN'T FALL INTO ENEMY HANDS.
WHAT A SHAME!
WE HAVE NO CHOICE! BISMARCK MUST NOT GET HIS HANDS ON THE AETHERITE! HANG ON, SERAPHIN!
SEE YOU AT THE RENDEZVOUS POINT?
NO! WE MAY NEED REINFORCEMENTS!
...GET EVERYONE IN THE BOAT AND MEET US AT THE MANOR!

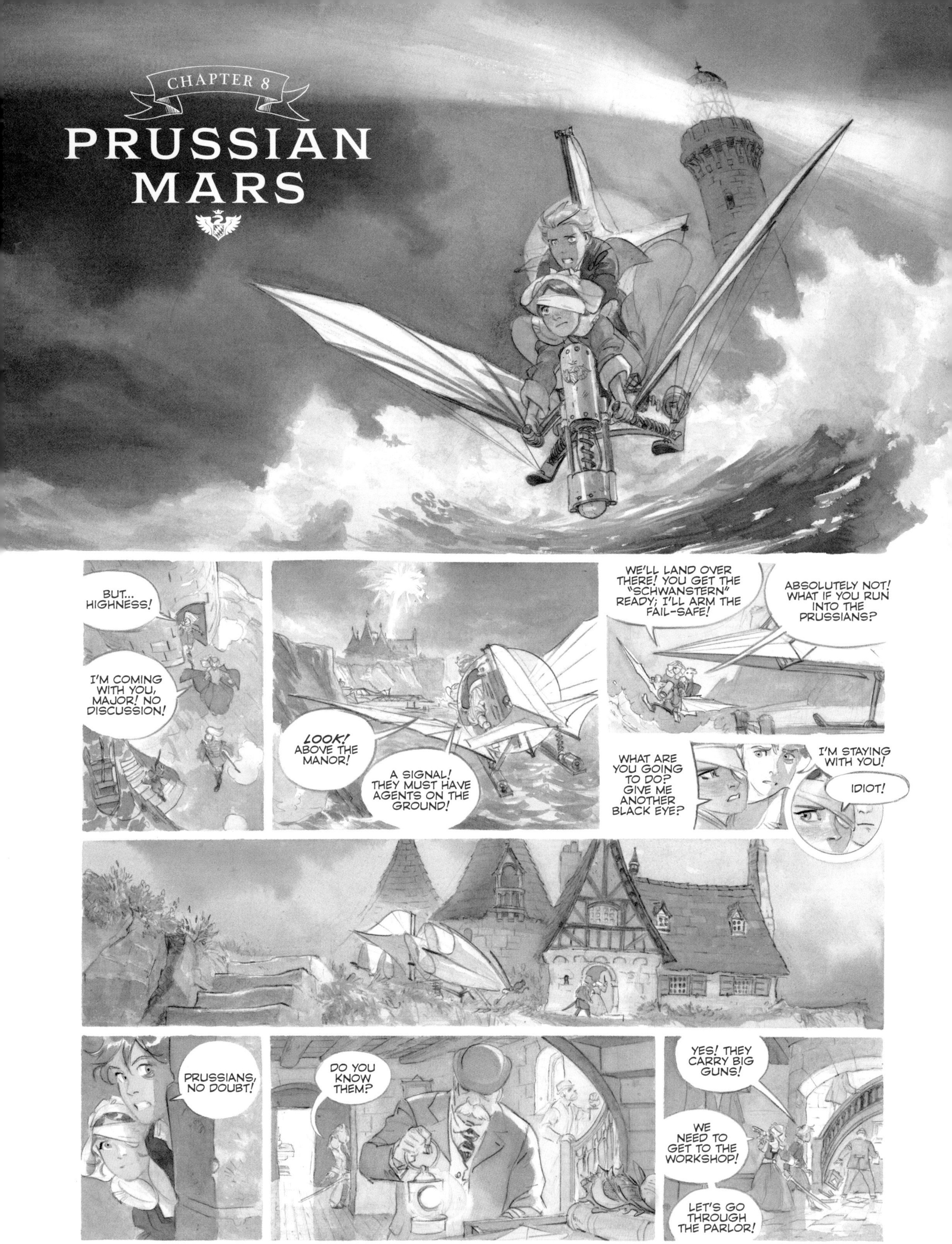
CHAPTER 8
PRUSSIAN MARS
BUT... HIGHNESS!
I'M COMING WITH YOU, MAJOR! NO DISCUSSION!
LOOK! ABOVE THE MANOR!
A SIGNAL! THEY MUST HAVE AGENTS ON THE GROUND!
WE'LL LAND OVER THERE! YOU GET THE "SCHWANSTERN" READY; I'LL ARM THE FAIL-SAFE!
ABSOLUTELY NOT! WHAT IF YOU RUN INTO THE PRUSSIANS?
WHAT ARE YOU GOING TO DO? GIVE ME ANOTHER BLACK EYE?
I'M STAYING WITH YOU!
IDIOT!
PRUSSIANS, NO DOUBT!
DO YOU KNOW THEM?
YES! THEY CARRY BIG GUNS!
WE NEED TO GET TO THE WORKSHOP!
LET'S GO THROUGH THE PARLOR!

SO FAR,
SO GOOD!

BLING
CRACK

THEY'RE
IN THE
KITCHEN!

WE'RE
SURROUNDED!

WHAT
SHOULD
WE DO?

GIVE ME
A BOOST!

EXCUSE
ME?

CLIMB UP
AND DO
WHAT I SAY!

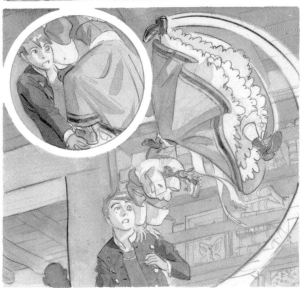

THERE'S
NO ONE HERE,
HERR
KOMMANDANT!

WELL THEN,
WHAT ARE
YOU WAITING
FOR?

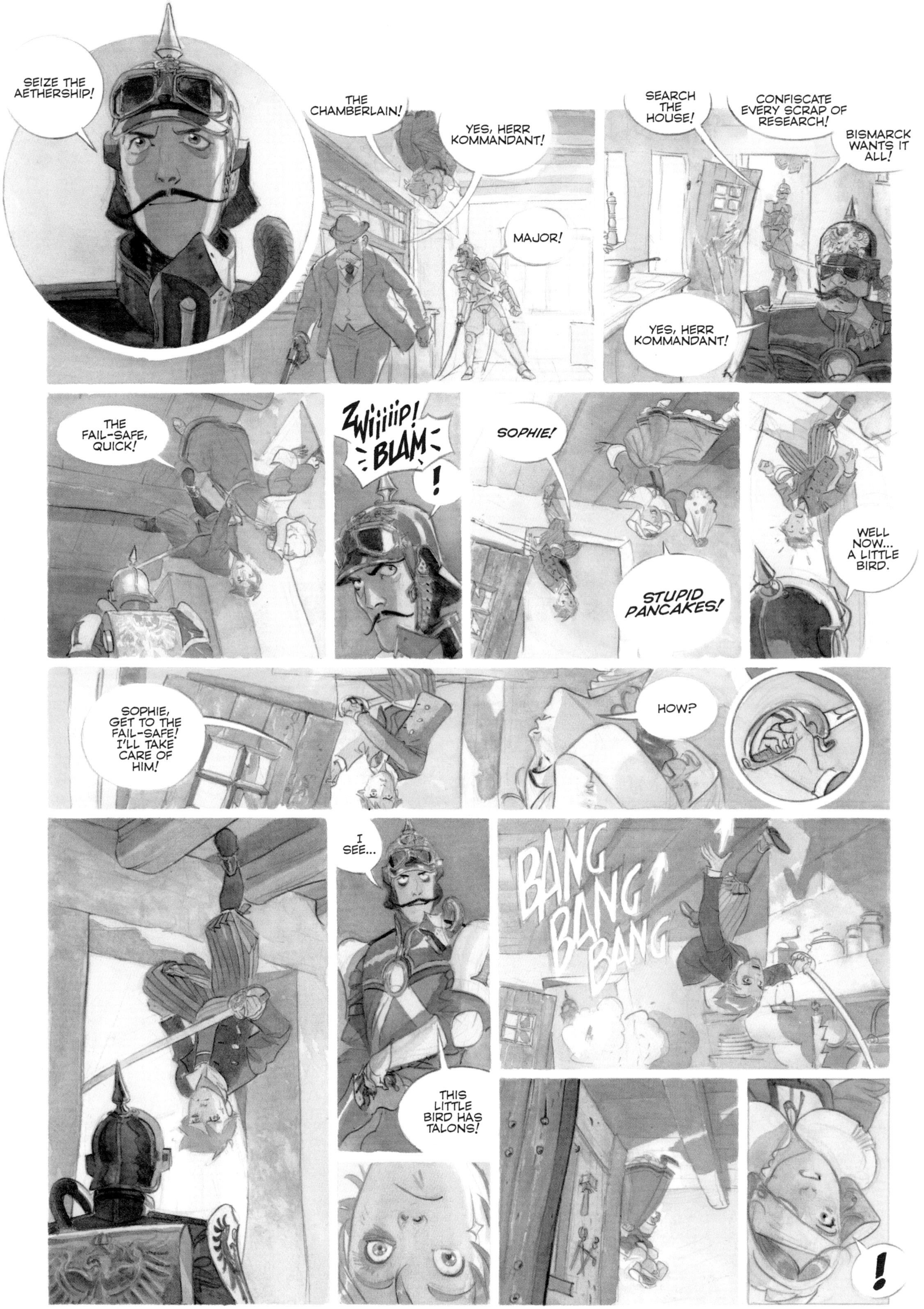
SEIZE THE AETHERSHIP!
THE CHAMBERLAIN!
YES, HERR KOMMANDANT!
MAJOR!
SEARCH THE HOUSE!
CONFISCATE EVERY SCRAP OF RESEARCH!
BISMARCK WANTS IT ALL!
YES, HERR KOMMANDANT!
THE FAIL-SAFE, QUICK!
ZWiiiiip! BLAM
!
SOPHIE!
STUPID PANCAKES!
WELL NOW... A LITTLE BIRD.
SOPHIE, GET TO THE FAIL-SAFE! I'LL TAKE CARE OF HIM!
HOW?
I SEE...
BANG BANG BANG
THIS LITTLE BIRD HAS TALONS!
!

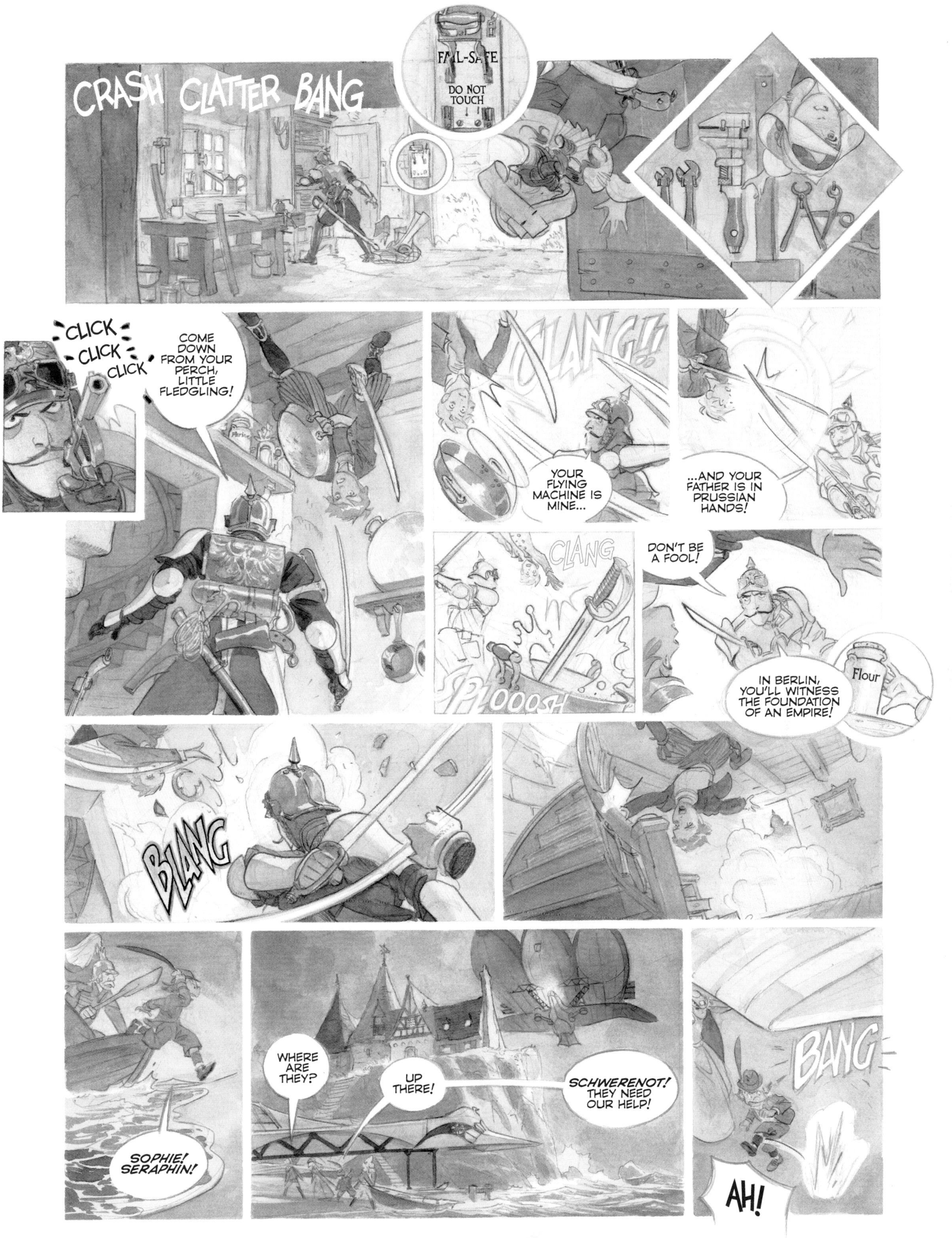

CRASH CLATTER BANG
FAIL-SAFE
DO NOT TOUCH
CLICK CLICK CLICK
COME DOWN FROM YOUR PERCH, LITTLE FLEDGLING!
CLANG!!
YOUR FLYING MACHINE IS MINE...
...AND YOUR FATHER IS IN PRUSSIAN HANDS!
CLANG
PLOOOSH
DON'T BE A FOOL!
Flour
IN BERLIN, YOU'LL WITNESS THE FOUNDATION OF AN EMPIRE!
BLANG
SOPHIE! SERAPHIN!
WHERE ARE THEY?
UP THERE!
SCHWERENOT! THEY NEED OUR HELP!
BANG
AH!

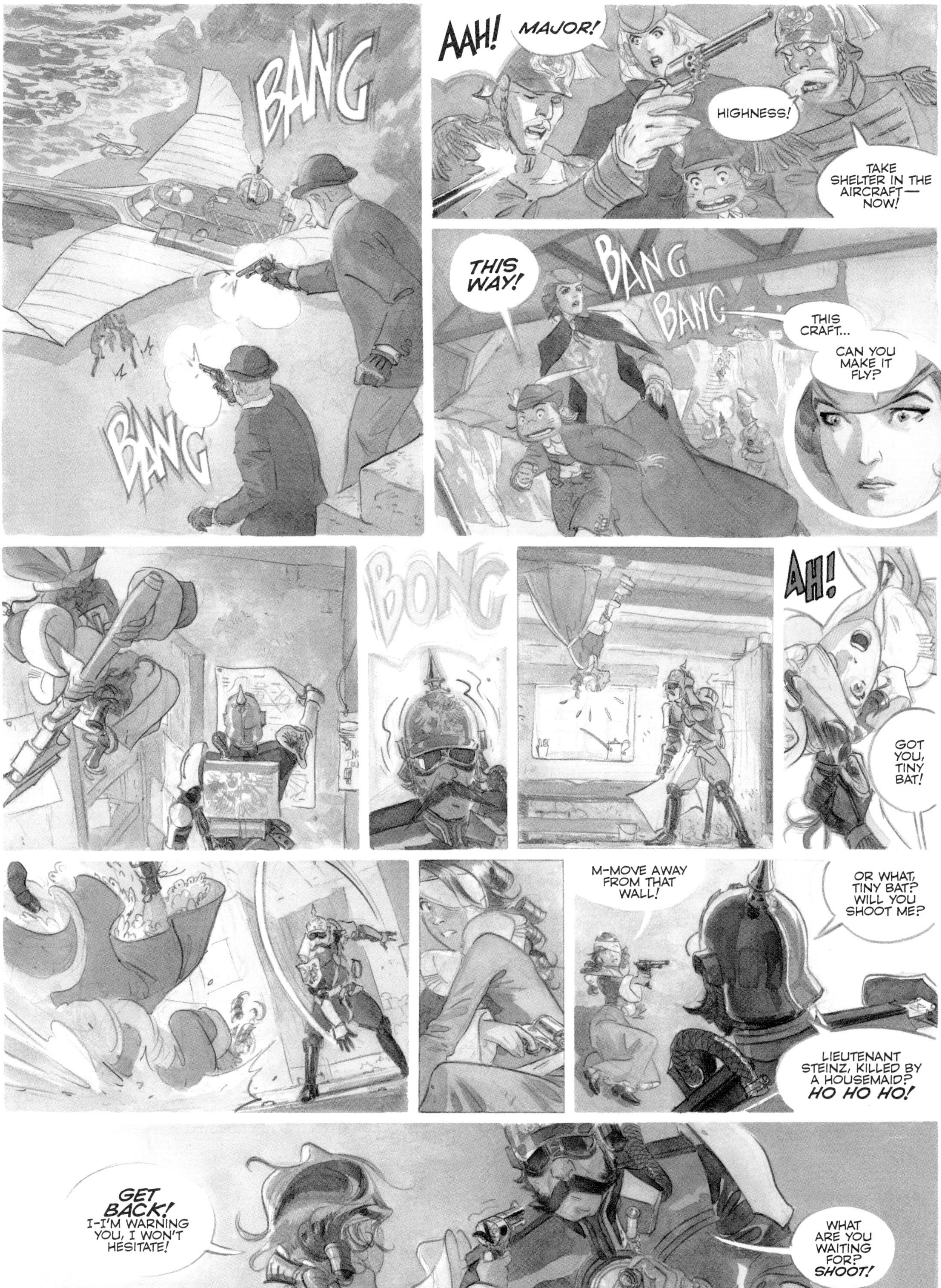
BANG
BANG
AAH!
MAJOR!
HIGHNESS!
TAKE SHELTER IN THE AIRCRAFT—NOW!
THIS WAY!
BANG
BANG
THIS CRAFT...
CAN YOU MAKE IT FLY?
BONG
AH!
GOT YOU, TINY BAT!
M-MOVE AWAY FROM THAT WALL!
OR WHAT, TINY BAT? WILL YOU SHOOT ME?
LIEUTENANT STEINZ, KILLED BY A HOUSEMAID? HO HO HO!
GET BACK! I-I'M WARNING YOU, I WON'T HESITATE!
WHAT ARE YOU WAITING FOR? SHOOT!

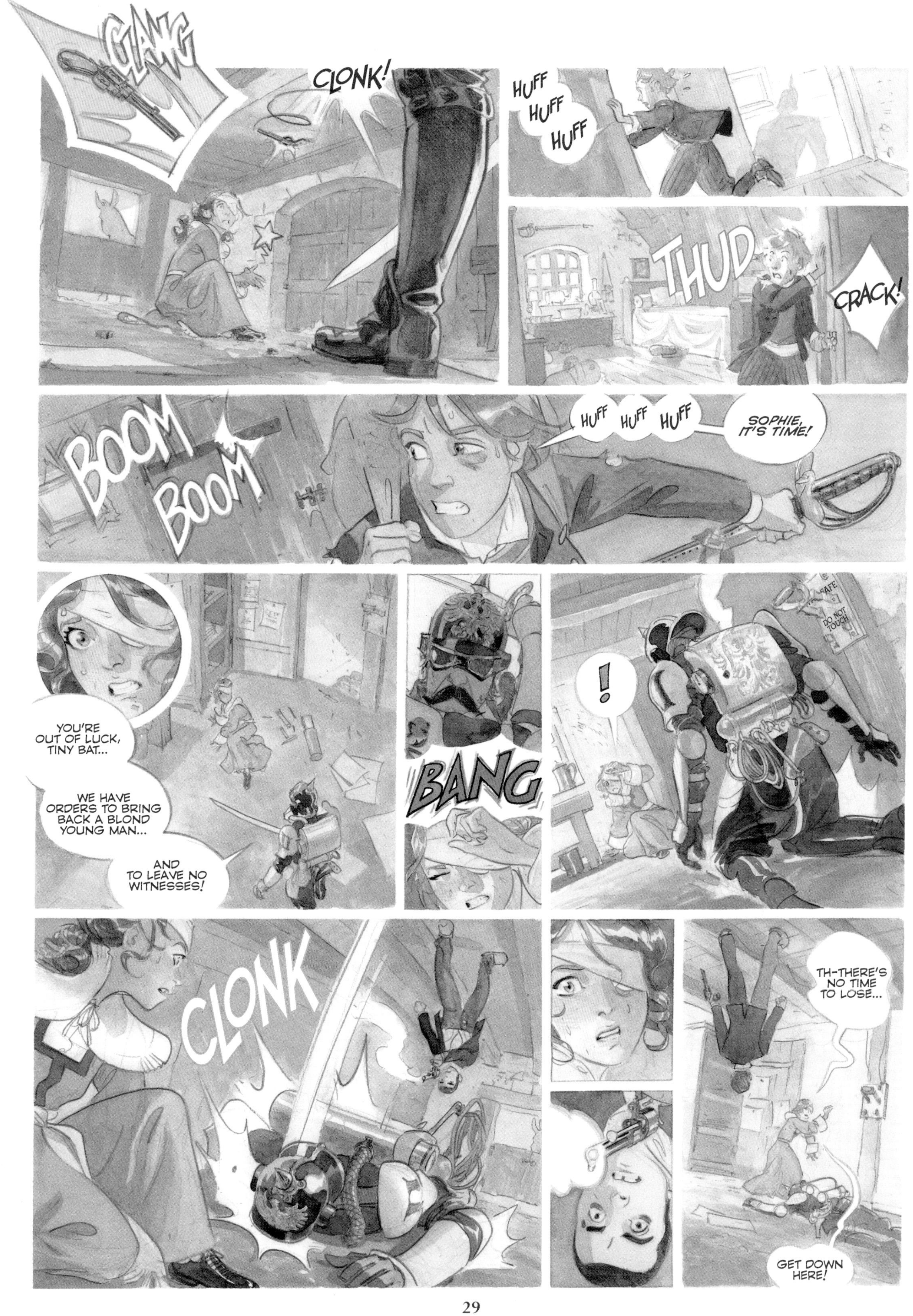
CLANG
CLONK!
HUFF
HUFF
HUFF
THUD
CRACK!
BOOM
BOOM
HUFF HUFF HUFF
SOPHIE, IT'S TIME!
YOU'RE OUT OF LUCK, TINY BAT...
WE HAVE ORDERS TO BRING BACK A BLOND YOUNG MAN...
AND TO LEAVE NO WITNESSES!
BANG
!
SAFE
DO NOT TOUCH
CLONK
TH-THERE'S NO TIME TO LOSE...
GET DOWN HERE!

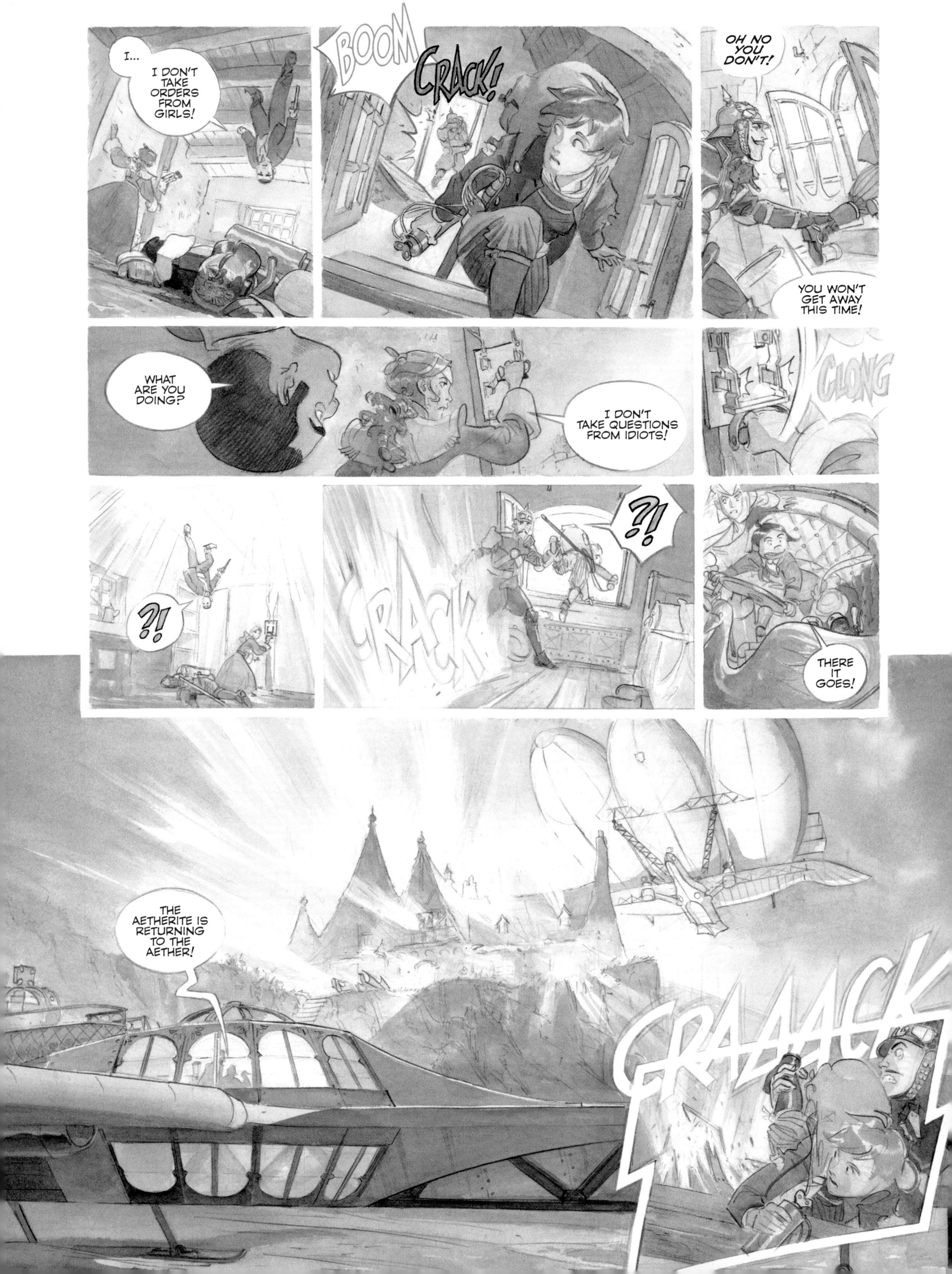

I...
I DON'T TAKE ORDERS FROM GIRLS!
BOOM
CRACK!
OH NO YOU DON'T!
YOU WON'T GET AWAY THIS TIME!
WHAT ARE YOU DOING?
I DON'T TAKE QUESTIONS FROM IDIOTS!
CLONG
?!
CRACK
?!
THERE IT GOES!
THE AETHERITE IS RETURNING TO THE AETHER!
CRAAACK

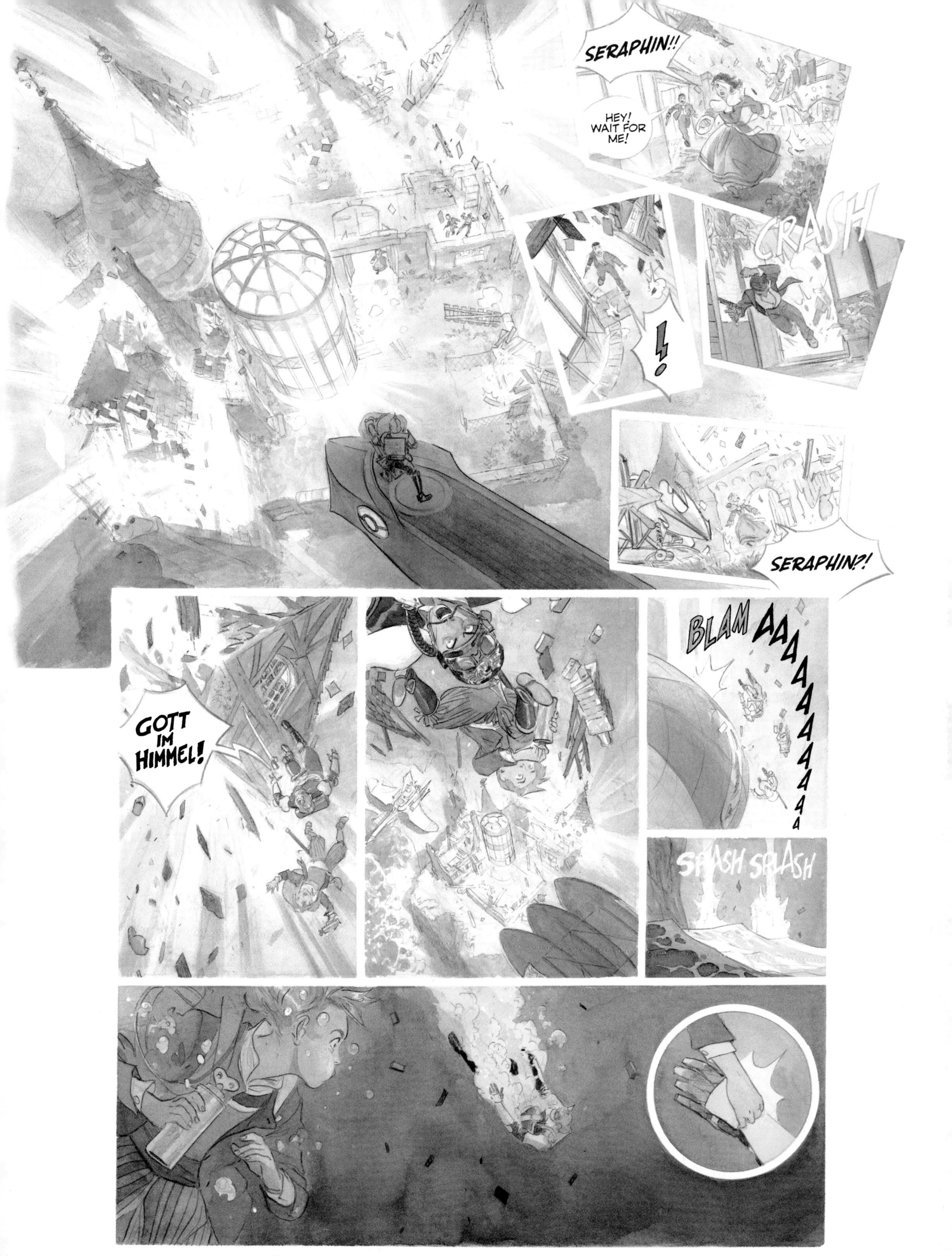
SERAPHIN!!
HEY! WAIT FOR ME!
CRASH
!
SERAPHIN?!
GOTT IM HIMMEL!
BLAM
AAAAAAAAAAAAA
SPLASH SPLASH

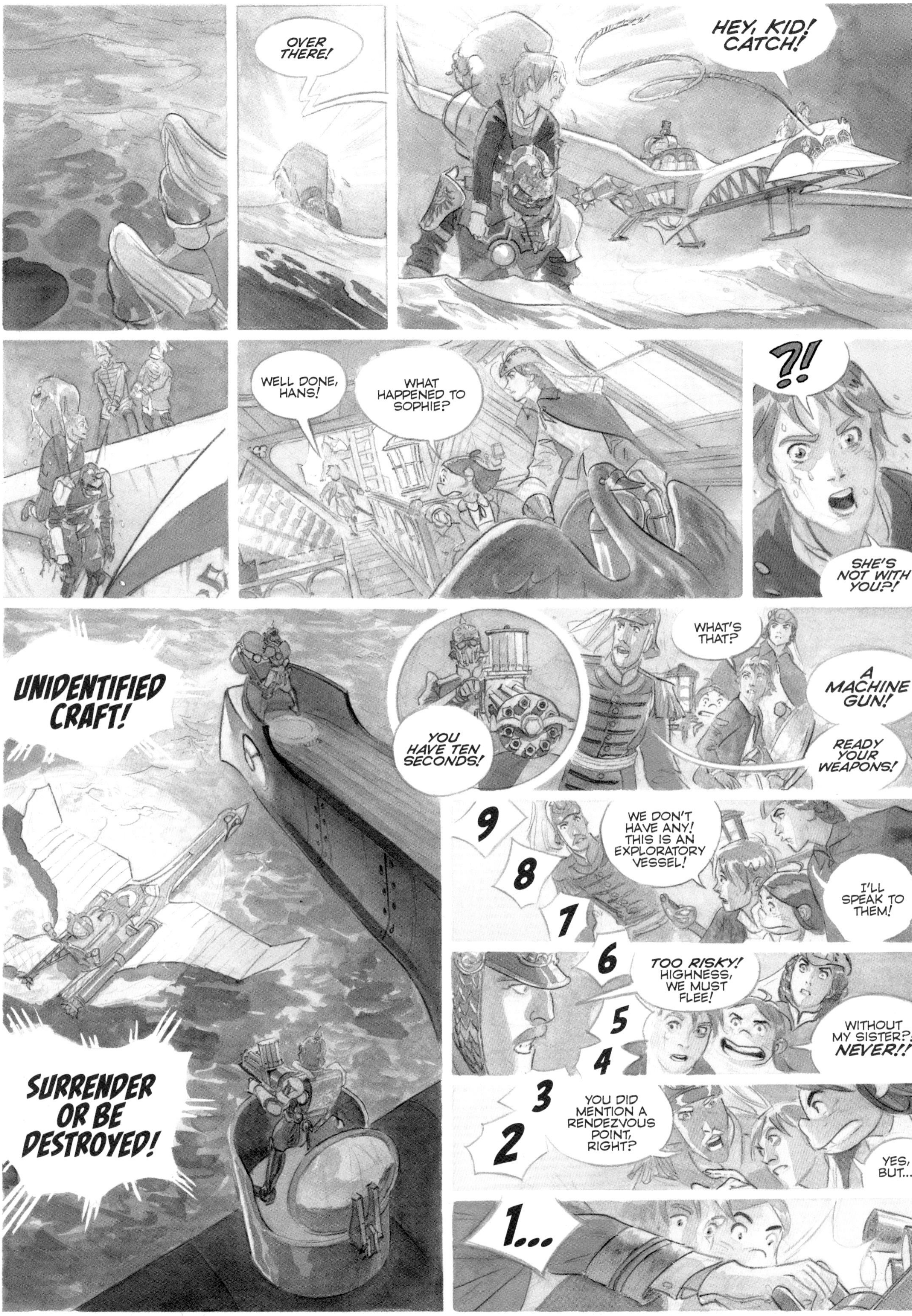
OVER THERE!
HEY, KID! CATCH!
WELL DONE, HANS!
WHAT HAPPENED TO SOPHIE?
?!
SHE'S NOT WITH YOU?!
UNIDENTIFIED CRAFT!
SURRENDER OR BE DESTROYED!
YOU HAVE TEN SECONDS!
WHAT'S THAT?
A MACHINE GUN!
READY YOUR WEAPONS!
9
8
WE DON'T HAVE ANY! THIS IS AN EXPLORATORY VESSEL!
7
I'LL SPEAK TO THEM!
6
TOO RISKY! HIGHNESS, WE MUST FLEE!
5
4
WITHOUT MY SISTER?! NEVER!!
3
2
YOU DID MENTION A RENDEZVOUS POINT, RIGHT?
YES, BUT...
1...

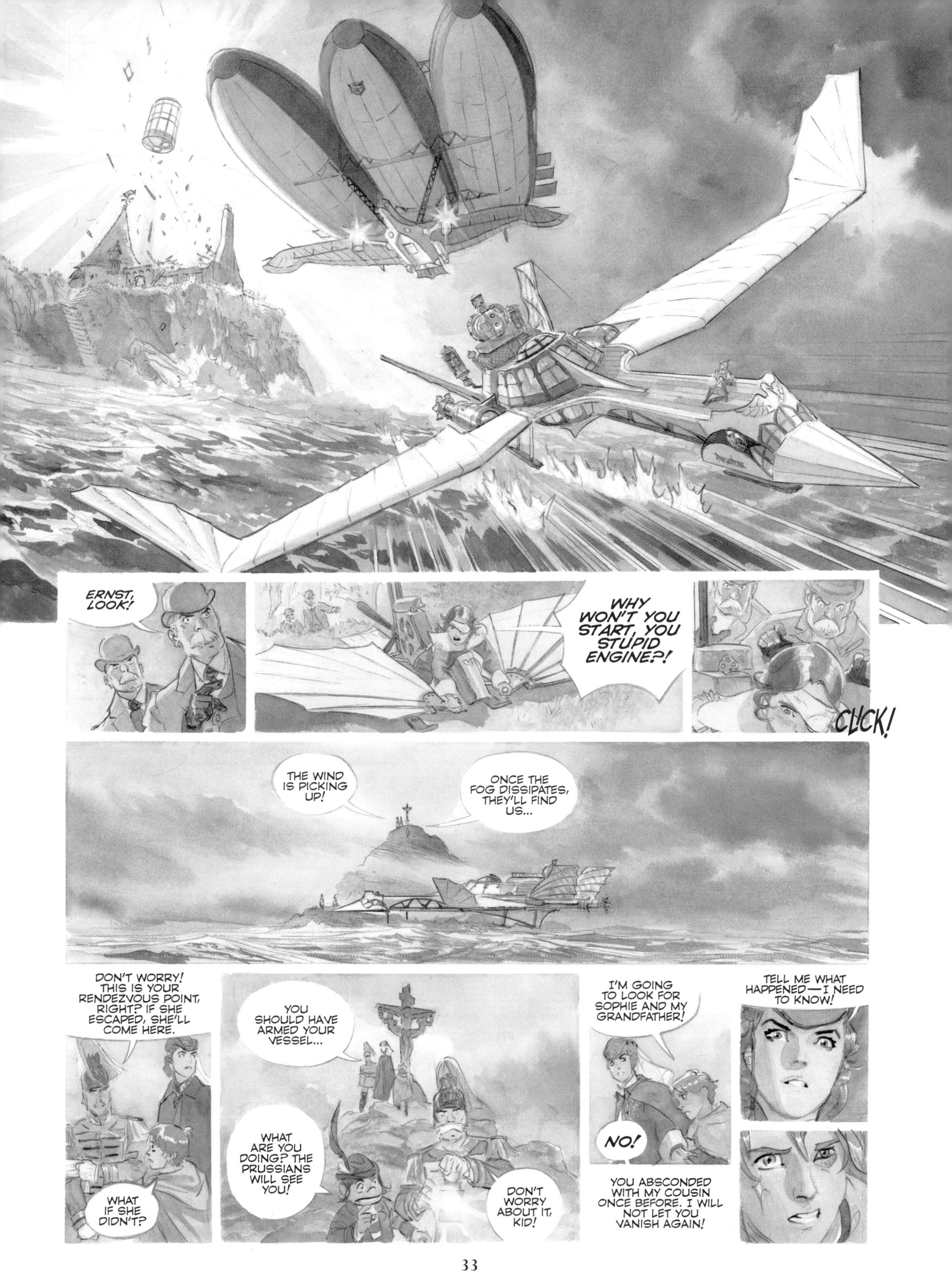
ERNST, LOOK!
WHY WON'T YOU START, YOU STUPID ENGINE?!
CLICK!
THE WIND IS PICKING UP!
ONCE THE FOG DISSIPATES, THEY'LL FIND US...
DON'T WORRY! THIS IS YOUR RENDEZVOUS POINT, RIGHT? IF SHE ESCAPED, SHE'LL COME HERE.
WHAT IF SHE DIDN'T?
YOU SHOULD HAVE ARMED YOUR VESSEL...
WHAT ARE YOU DOING? THE PRUSSIANS WILL SEE YOU!
DON'T WORRY ABOUT IT, KID!
I'M GOING TO LOOK FOR SOPHIE AND MY GRANDFATHER!
NO!
YOU ABSCONDED WITH MY COUSIN ONCE BEFORE. I WILL NOT LET YOU VANISH AGAIN!
TELL ME WHAT HAPPENED—I NEED TO KNOW!

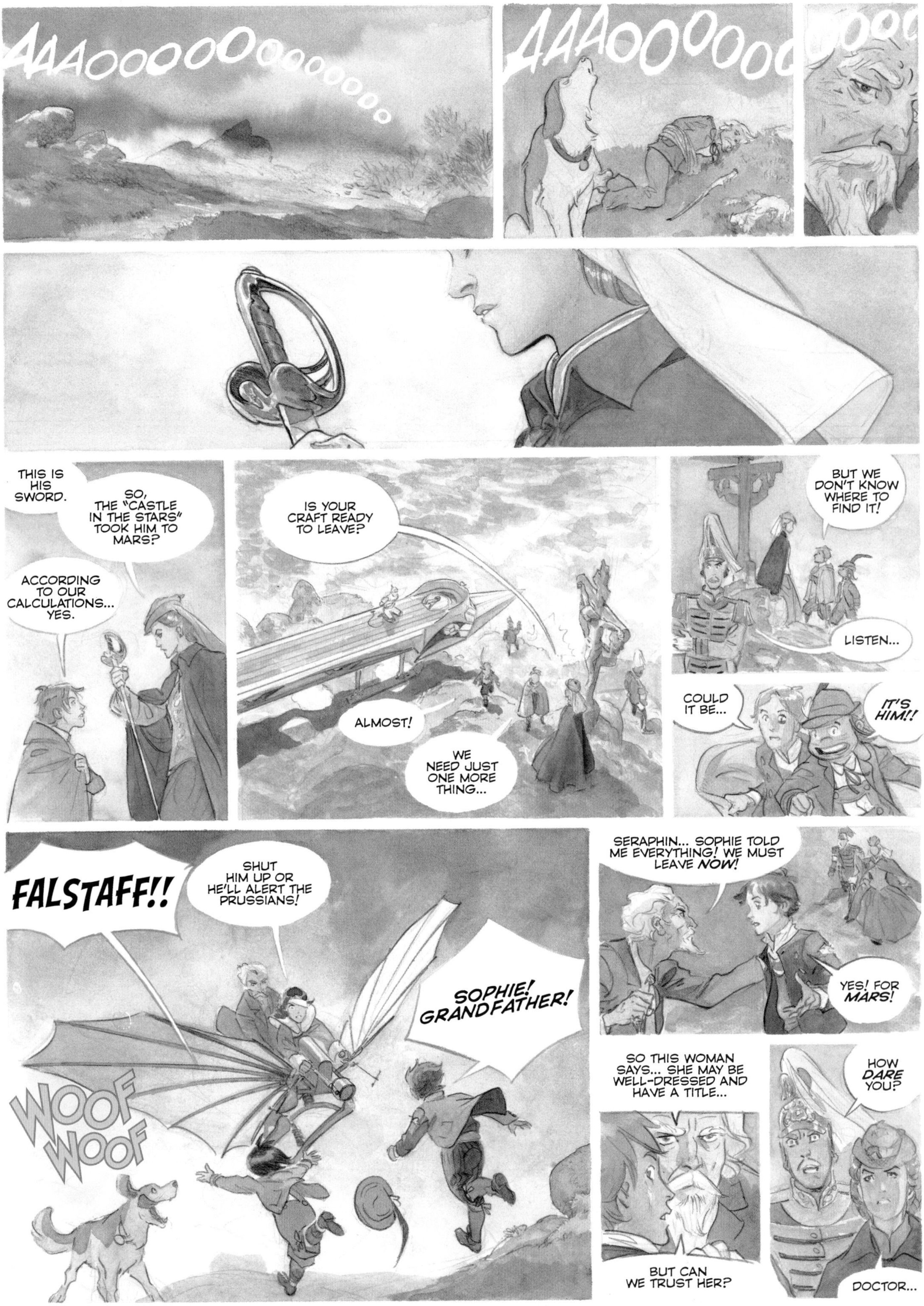
AAAOOOOOOOOOOOOOOO
AAAOOOOOOOO
THIS IS HIS SWORD.
SO, THE "CASTLE IN THE STARS" TOOK HIM TO MARS?
ACCORDING TO OUR CALCULATIONS... YES.
IS YOUR CRAFT READY TO LEAVE?
ALMOST!
WE NEED JUST ONE MORE THING...
BUT WE DON'T KNOW WHERE TO FIND IT!
LISTEN...
COULD IT BE...
IT'S HIM!!
FALSTAFF!!
SHUT HIM UP OR HE'LL ALERT THE PRUSSIANS!
SOPHIE! GRANDFATHER!
WOOF WOOF
SERAPHIN... SOPHIE TOLD ME EVERYTHING! WE MUST LEAVE NOW!
YES! FOR MARS!
SO THIS WOMAN SAYS... SHE MAY BE WELL-DRESSED AND HAVE A TITLE...
BUT CAN WE TRUST HER?
HOW DARE YOU?
DOCTOR...

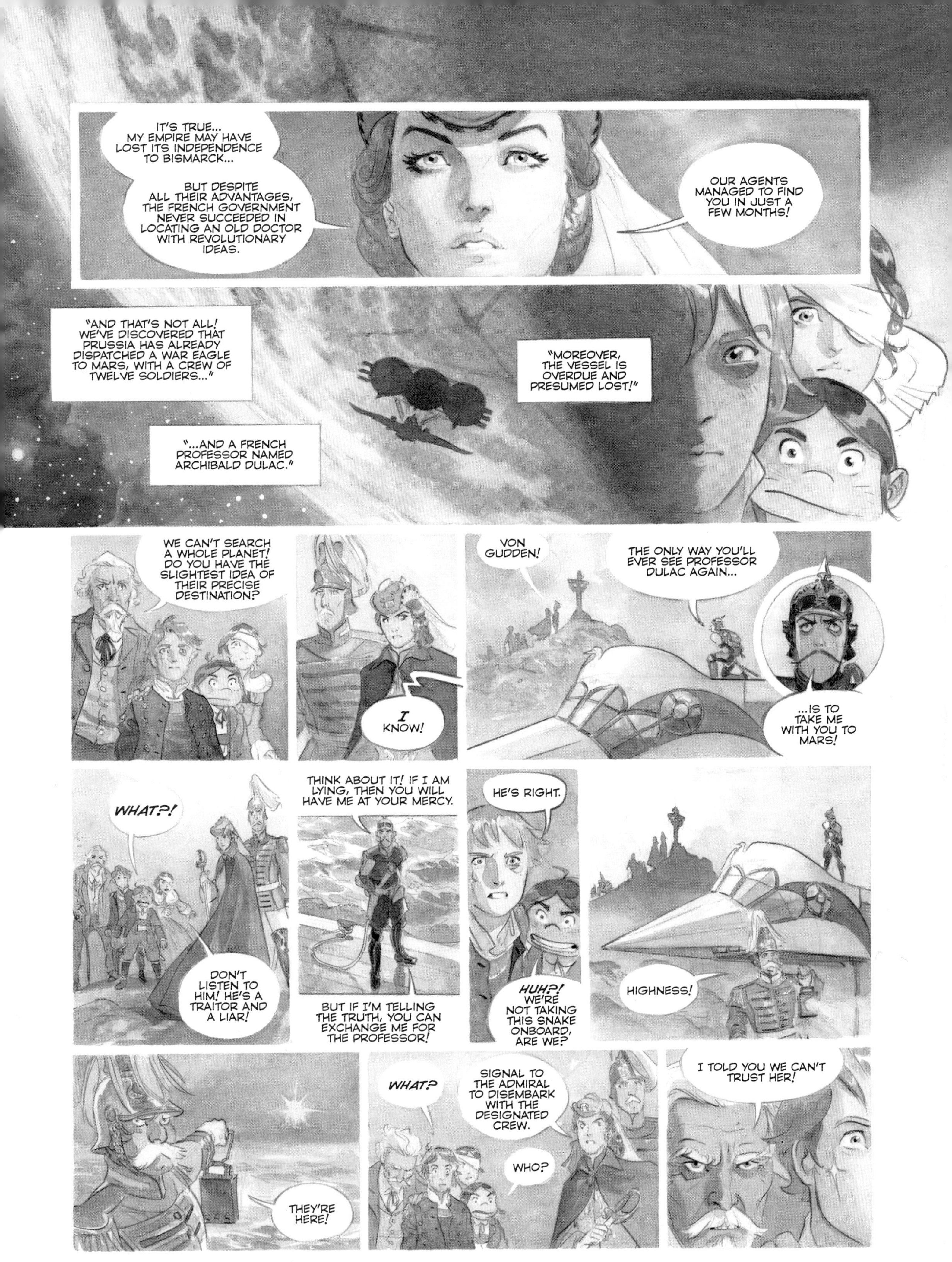

IT'S TRUE... MY EMPIRE MAY HAVE LOST ITS INDEPENDENCE TO BISMARCK...
BUT DESPITE ALL THEIR ADVANTAGES, THE FRENCH GOVERNMENT NEVER SUCCEEDED IN LOCATING AN OLD DOCTOR WITH REVOLUTIONARY IDEAS.
OUR AGENTS MANAGED TO FIND YOU IN JUST A FEW MONTHS!
"AND THAT'S NOT ALL! WE'VE DISCOVERED THAT PRUSSIA HAS ALREADY DISPATCHED A WAR EAGLE TO MARS, WITH A CREW OF TWELVE SOLDIERS..."
"...AND A FRENCH PROFESSOR NAMED ARCHIBALD DULAC."
"MOREOVER, THE VESSEL IS OVERDUE AND PRESUMED LOST!"
WE CAN'T SEARCH A WHOLE PLANET! DO YOU HAVE THE SLIGHTEST IDEA OF THEIR PRECISE DESTINATION?
I KNOW!
VON GUDDEN!
THE ONLY WAY YOU'LL EVER SEE PROFESSOR DULAC AGAIN...
...IS TO TAKE ME WITH YOU TO MARS!
WHAT?!
DON'T LISTEN TO HIM! HE'S A TRAITOR AND A LIAR!
THINK ABOUT IT! IF I AM LYING, THEN YOU WILL HAVE ME AT YOUR MERCY.
BUT IF I'M TELLING THE TRUTH, YOU CAN EXCHANGE ME FOR THE PROFESSOR!
HE'S RIGHT.
HUH?! WE'RE NOT TAKING THIS SNAKE ONBOARD, ARE WE?
HIGHNESS!
THEY'RE HERE!
WHAT?
SIGNAL TO THE ADMIRAL TO DISEMBARK WITH THE DESIGNATED CREW.
WHO?
I TOLD YOU WE CAN'T TRUST HER!

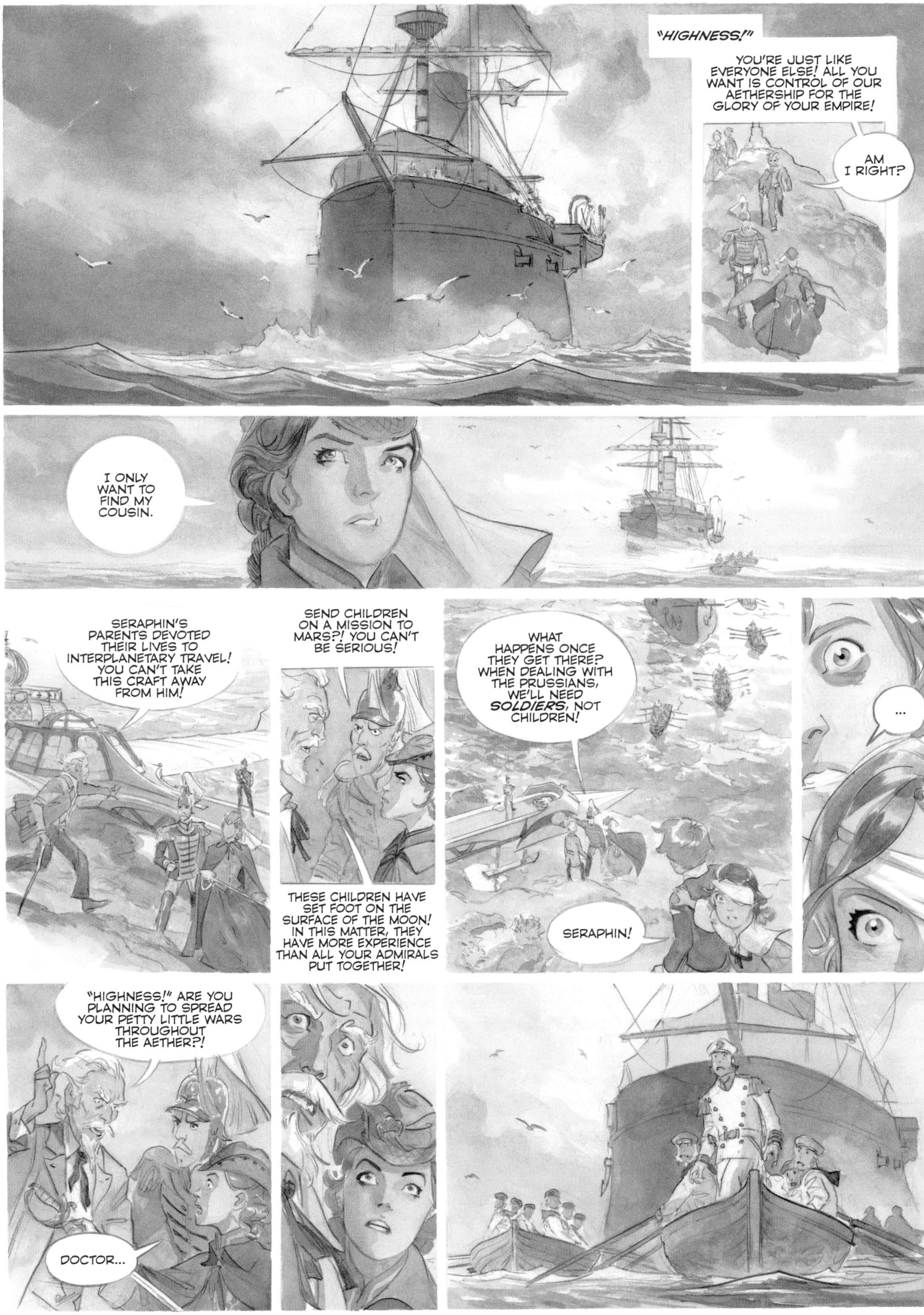

"HIGHNESS!"
YOU'RE JUST LIKE EVERYONE ELSE! ALL YOU WANT IS CONTROL OF OUR AETHERSHIP FOR THE GLORY OF YOUR EMPIRE!
AM I RIGHT?
I ONLY WANT TO FIND MY COUSIN.
SERAPHIN'S PARENTS DEVOTED THEIR LIVES TO INTERPLANETARY TRAVEL! YOU CAN'T TAKE THIS CRAFT AWAY FROM HIM!
SEND CHILDREN ON A MISSION TO MARS?! YOU CAN'T BE SERIOUS!
THESE CHILDREN HAVE SET FOOT ON THE SURFACE OF THE MOON! IN THIS MATTER, THEY HAVE MORE EXPERIENCE THAN ALL YOUR ADMIRALS PUT TOGETHER!
WHAT HAPPENS ONCE THEY GET THERE? WHEN DEALING WITH THE PRUSSIANS, WE'LL NEED SOLDIERS, NOT CHILDREN!
SERAPHIN!
...
"HIGHNESS!" ARE YOU PLANNING TO SPREAD YOUR PETTY LITTLE WARS THROUGHOUT THE AETHER?!
DOCTOR...

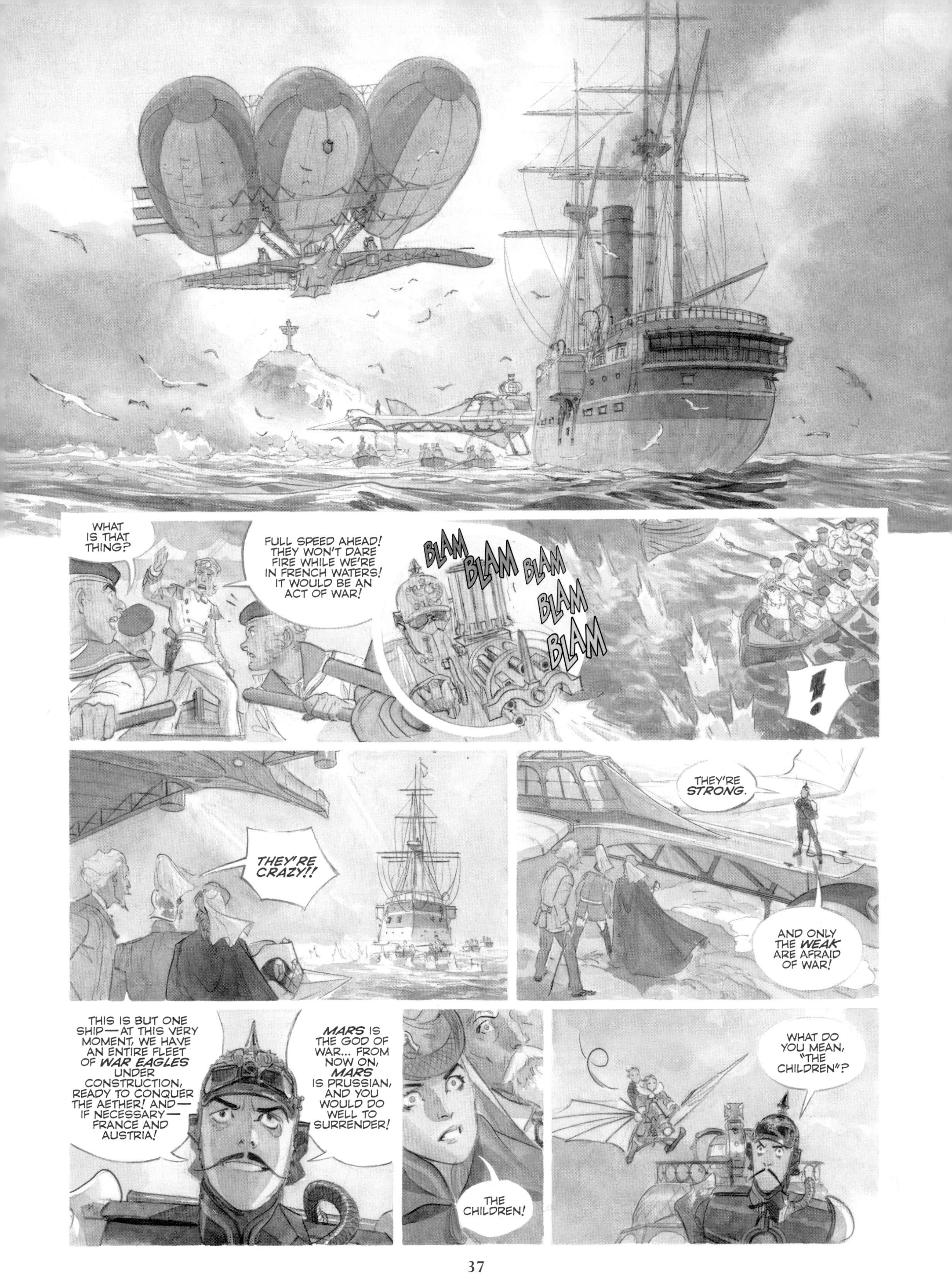
WHAT IS THAT THING?
FULL SPEED AHEAD! THEY WON'T DARE FIRE WHILE WE'RE IN FRENCH WATERS! IT WOULD BE AN ACT OF WAR!
BLAM BLAM BLAM BLAM BLAM
!
THEY'RE CRAZY!!
THEY'RE STRONG.
AND ONLY THE WEAK ARE AFRAID OF WAR!
THIS IS BUT ONE SHIP—AT THIS VERY MOMENT, WE HAVE AN ENTIRE FLEET OF WAR EAGLES UNDER CONSTRUCTION, READY TO CONQUER THE AETHER! AND—IF NECESSARY—FRANCE AND AUSTRIA!
MARS IS THE GOD OF WAR... FROM NOW ON, MARS IS PRUSSIAN, AND YOU WOULD DO WELL TO SURRENDER!
THE CHILDREN!
WHAT DO YOU MEAN, "THE CHILDREN"?

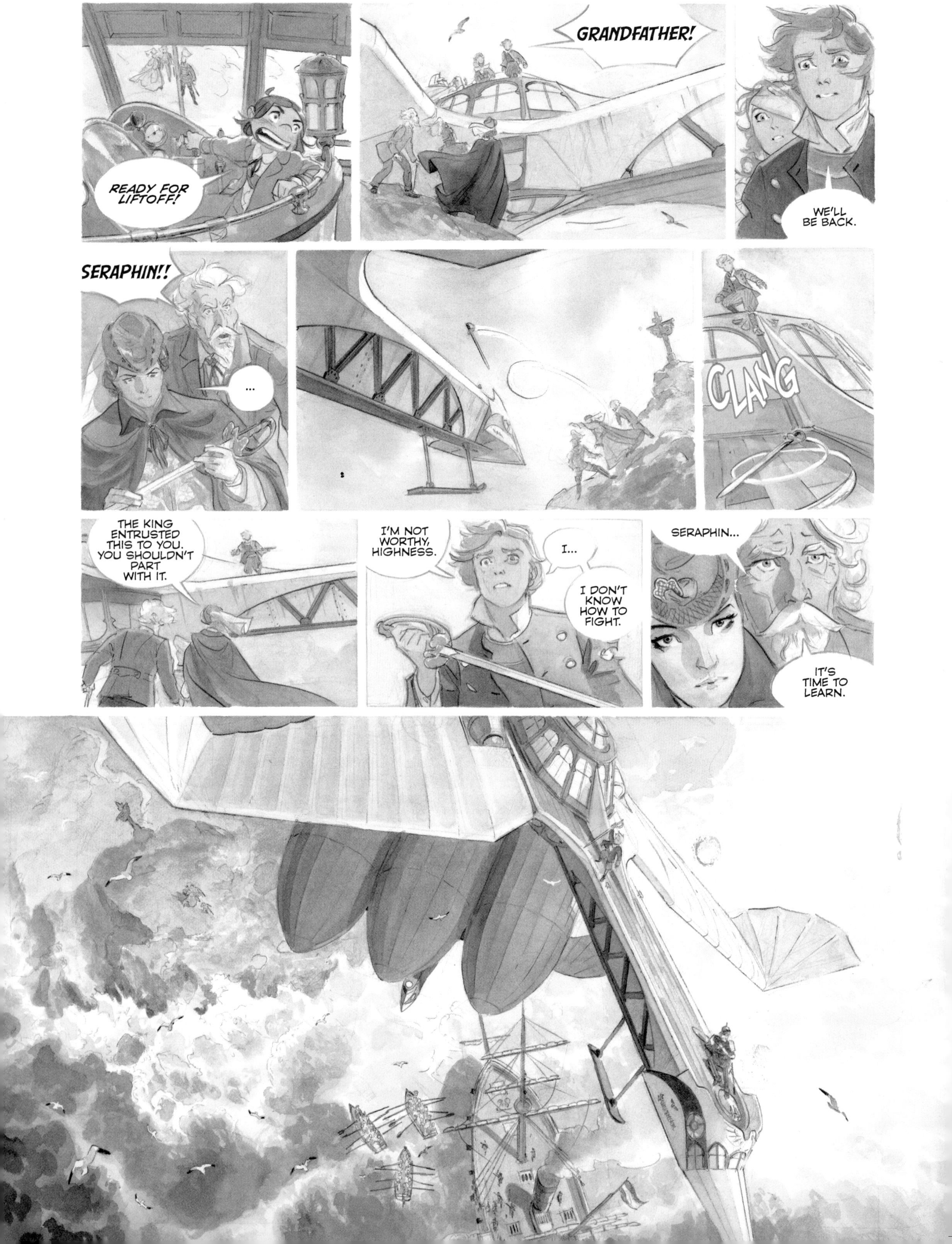
READY FOR LIFTOFF!
GRANDFATHER!
WE'LL BE BACK.
SERAPHIN!!
...
CLANG
THE KING ENTRUSTED THIS TO YOU. YOU SHOULDN'T PART WITH IT.
I'M NOT WORTHY, HIGHNESS.
I...
I DON'T KNOW HOW TO FIGHT.
SERAPHIN...
IT'S TIME TO LEARN.

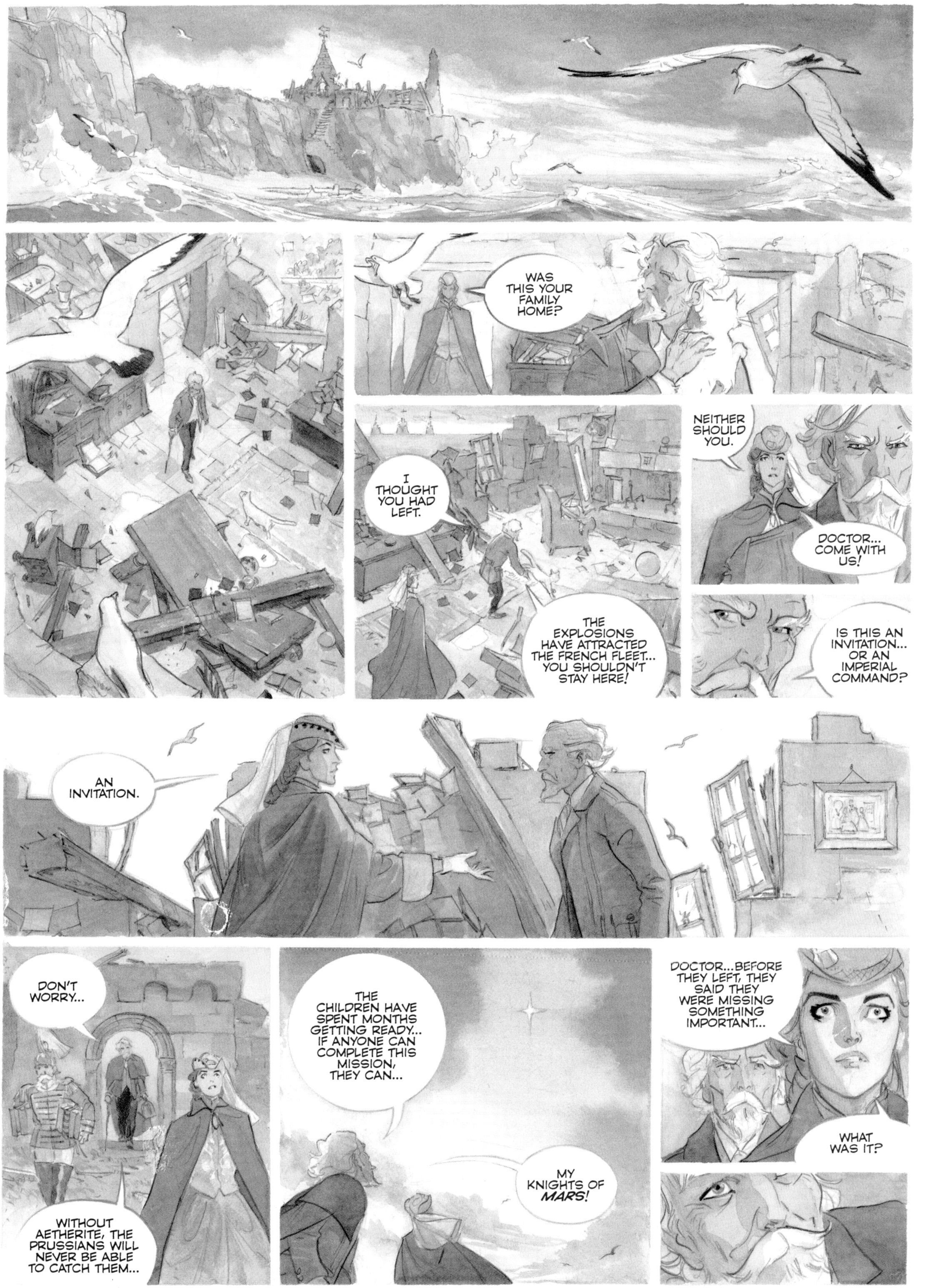
WAS THIS YOUR FAMILY HOME?
I THOUGHT YOU HAD LEFT.
NEITHER SHOULD YOU.
DOCTOR... COME WITH US!
THE EXPLOSIONS HAVE ATTRACTED THE FRENCH FLEET... YOU SHOULDN'T STAY HERE!
IS THIS AN INVITATION... OR AN IMPERIAL COMMAND?
AN INVITATION.
DON'T WORRY...
WITHOUT AETHERITE, THE PRUSSIANS WILL NEVER BE ABLE TO CATCH THEM...
THE CHILDREN HAVE SPENT MONTHS GETTING READY... IF ANYONE CAN COMPLETE THIS MISSION, THEY CAN...
MY KNIGHTS OF MARS!
DOCTOR...BEFORE THEY LEFT, THEY SAID THEY WERE MISSING SOMETHING IMPORTANT...
WHAT WAS IT?

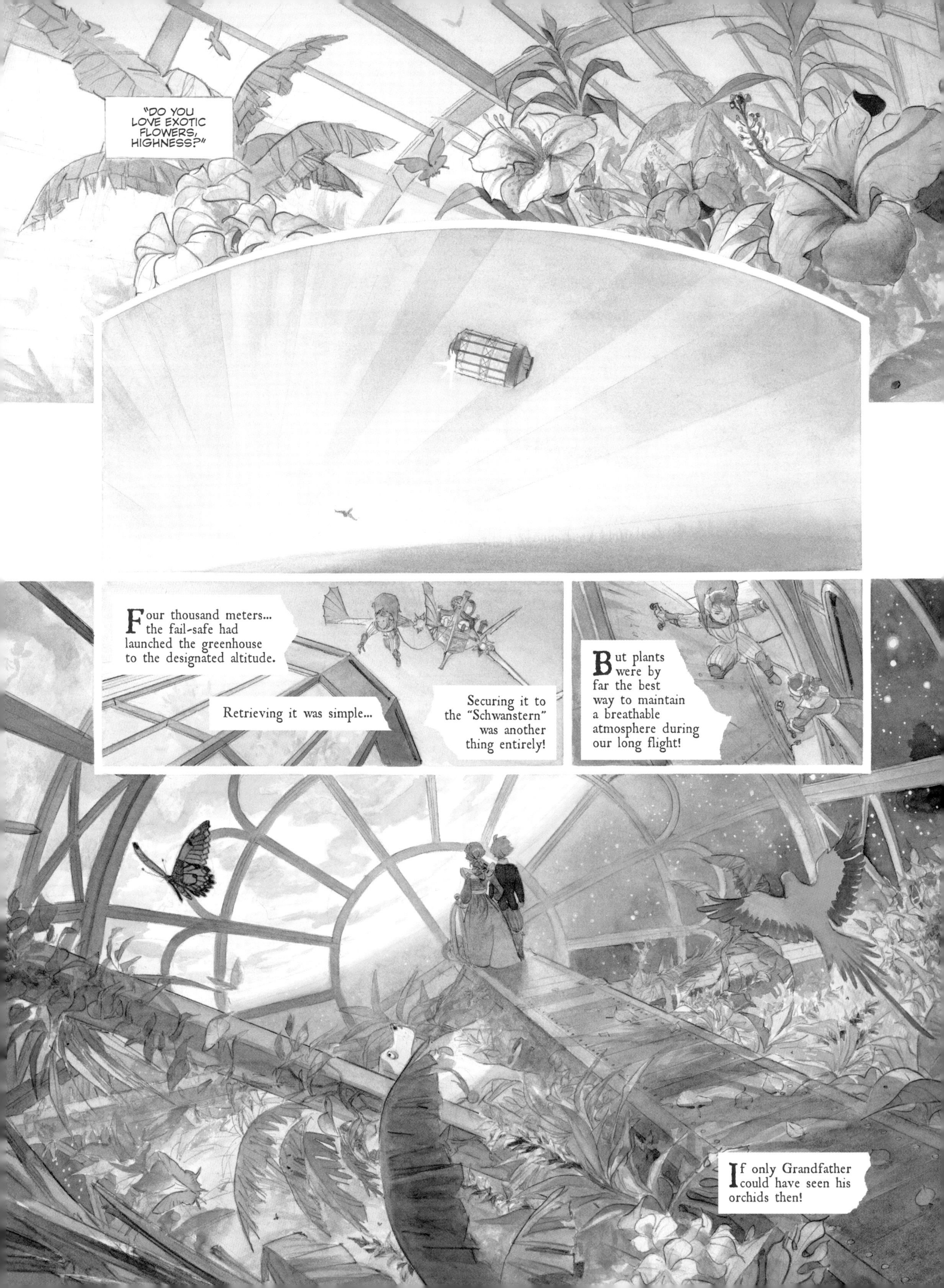
"DO YOU LOVE EXOTIC FLOWERS, HIGHNESS?"
Four thousand meters... the fail-safe had launched the greenhouse to the designated altitude.
Retrieving it was simple...
Securing it to the "Schwanstern" was another thing entirely!
But plants were by far the best way to maintain a breathable atmosphere during our long flight!
If only Grandfather could have seen his orchids then!

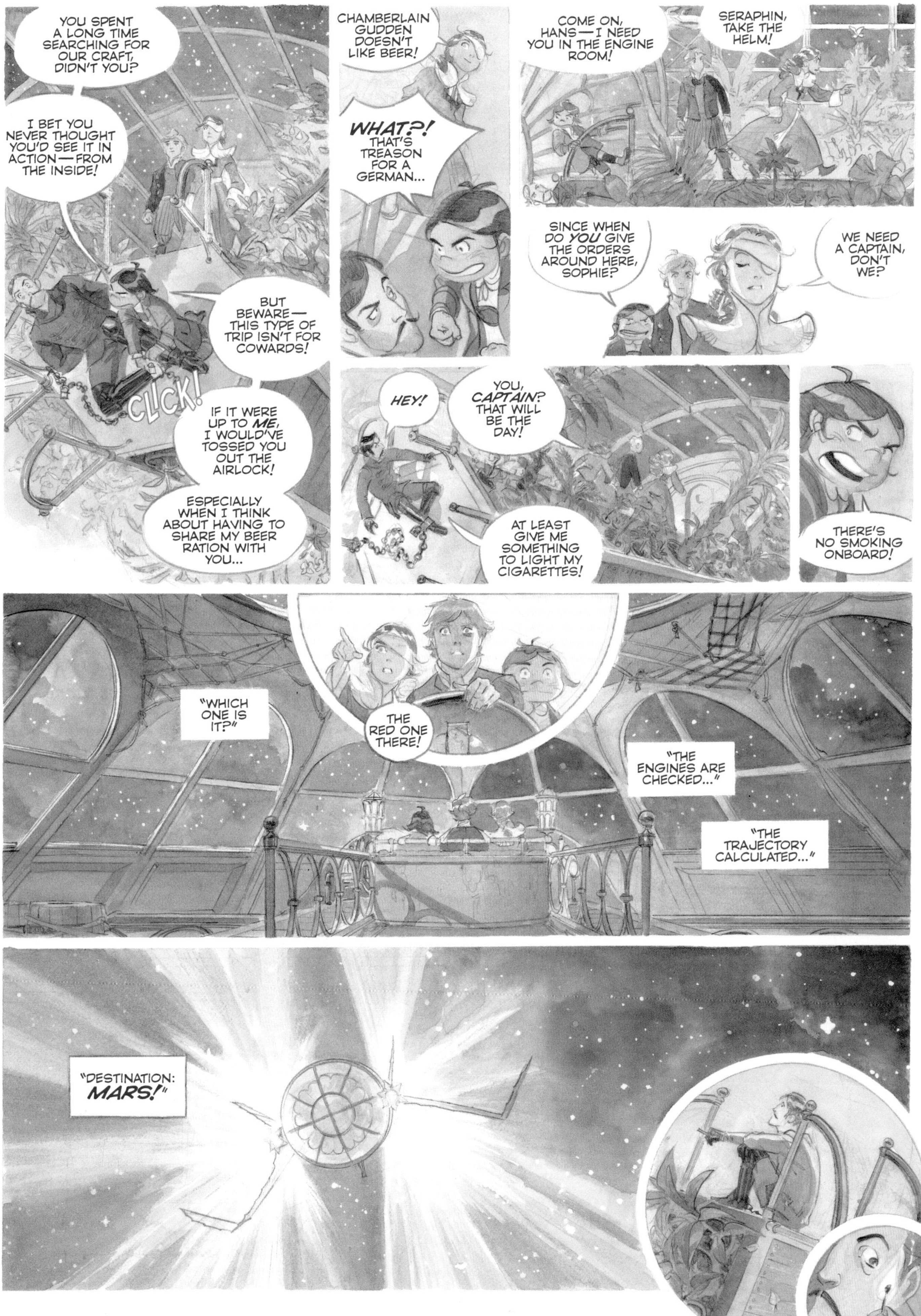
YOU SPENT A LONG TIME SEARCHING FOR OUR CRAFT, DIDN'T YOU?
I BET YOU NEVER THOUGHT YOU'D SEE IT IN ACTION—FROM THE INSIDE!
BUT BEWARE—THIS TYPE OF TRIP ISN'T FOR COWARDS!
CLICK!
IF IT WERE UP TO ME, I WOULD'VE TOSSED YOU OUT THE AIRLOCK!
ESPECIALLY WHEN I THINK ABOUT HAVING TO SHARE MY BEER RATION WITH YOU...
CHAMBERLAIN GUDDEN DOESN'T LIKE BEER!
WHAT?! THAT'S TREASON FOR A GERMAN...
COME ON, HANS—I NEED YOU IN THE ENGINE ROOM!
SERAPHIN, TAKE THE HELM!
SINCE WHEN DO YOU GIVE THE ORDERS AROUND HERE, SOPHIE?
WE NEED A CAPTAIN, DON'T WE?
HEY!
YOU, CAPTAIN? THAT WILL BE THE DAY!
AT LEAST GIVE ME SOMETHING TO LIGHT MY CIGARETTES!
THERE'S NO SMOKING ONBOARD!
"WHICH ONE IS IT?"
THE RED ONE THERE!
"THE ENGINES ARE CHECKED..."
"THE TRAJECTORY CALCULATED..."
"DESTINATION: MARS!"

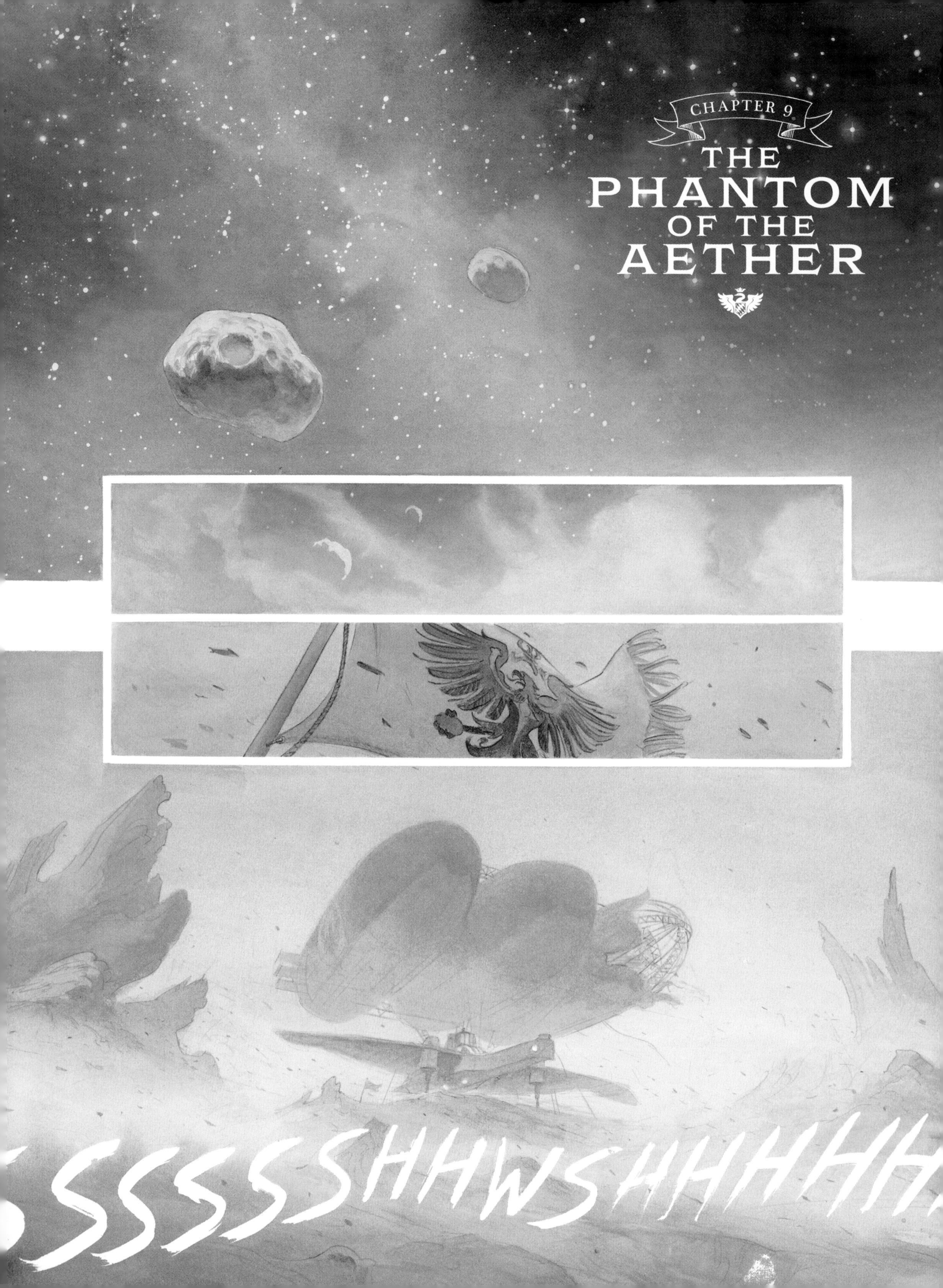
CHAPTER 9
THE PHANTOM OF THE AETHER
SSSSSSHHWSHHHHH

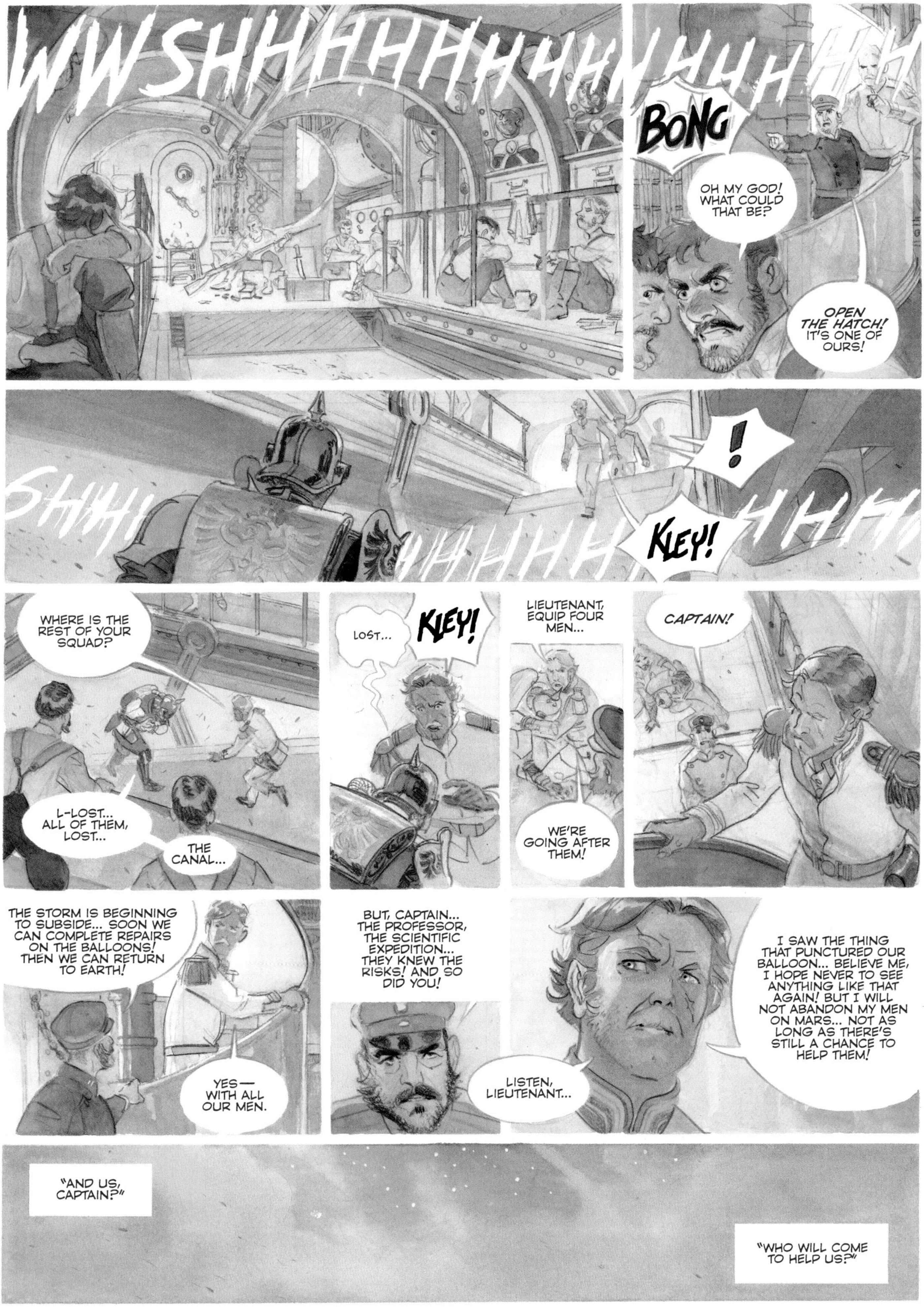
WWSHHHHHHHHHHHHHHHHHH
BONG
OH MY GOD! WHAT COULD THAT BE?
OPEN THE HATCH! IT'S ONE OF OURS!
SHHHHHHHHHHHHHHHHHM
!
KLEY!
WHERE IS THE REST OF YOUR SQUAD?
L-LOST... ALL OF THEM, LOST...
THE CANAL...
LOST...
KLEY!
LIEUTENANT, EQUIP FOUR MEN...
WE'RE GOING AFTER THEM!
CAPTAIN!
THE STORM IS BEGINNING TO SUBSIDE... SOON WE CAN COMPLETE REPAIRS ON THE BALLOONS! THEN WE CAN RETURN TO EARTH!
YES— WITH ALL OUR MEN.
BUT, CAPTAIN... THE PROFESSOR, THE SCIENTIFIC EXPEDITION... THEY KNEW THE RISKS! AND SO DID YOU!
LISTEN, LIEUTENANT...
I SAW THE THING THAT PUNCTURED OUR BALLOON... BELIEVE ME, I HOPE NEVER TO SEE ANYTHING LIKE THAT AGAIN! BUT I WILL NOT ABANDON MY MEN ON MARS... NOT AS LONG AS THERE'S STILL A CHANCE TO HELP THEM!
"AND US, CAPTAIN?"
"WHO WILL COME TO HELP US?"

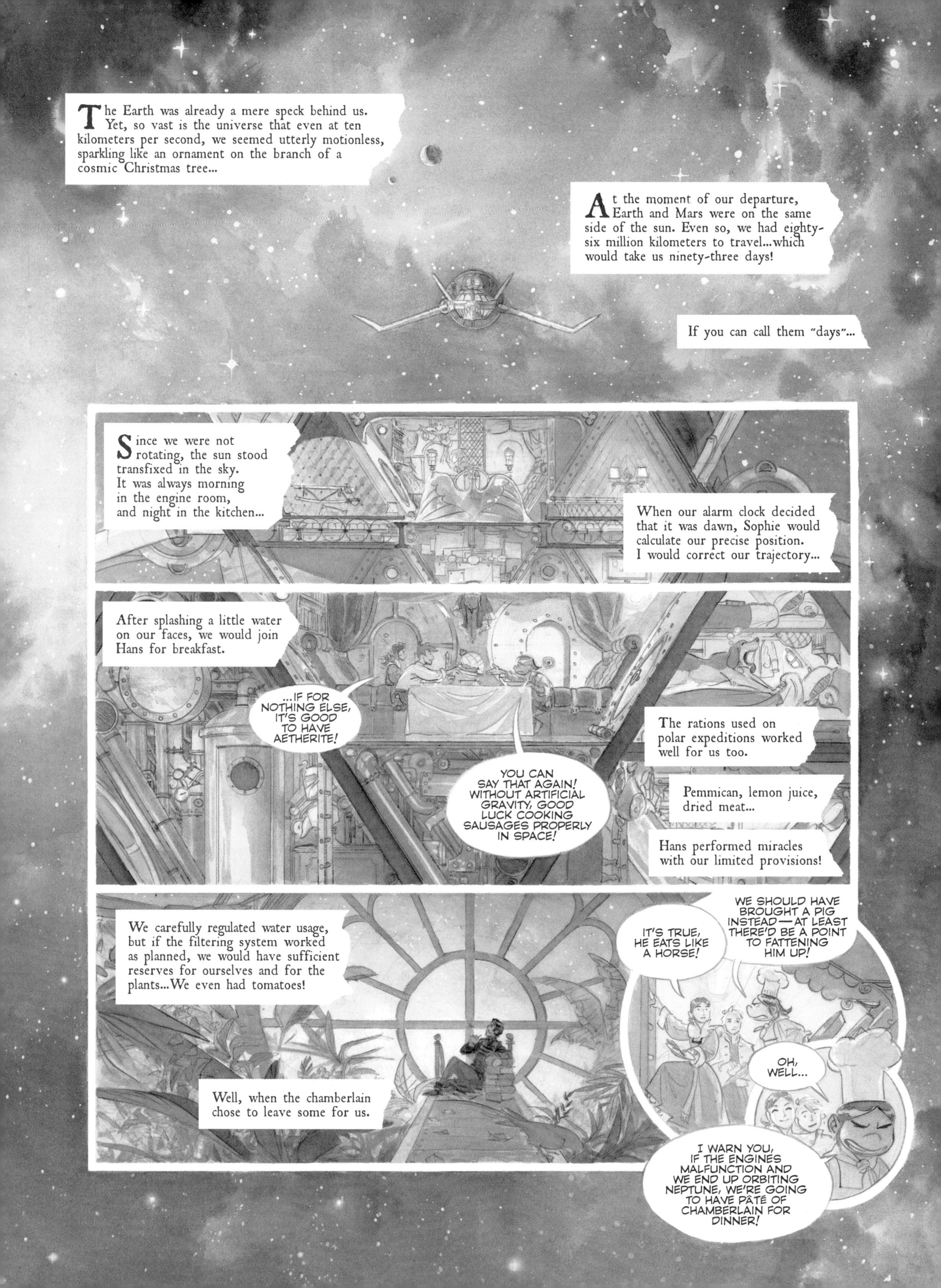
The Earth was already a mere speck behind us. Yet, so vast is the universe that even at ten kilometers per second, we seemed utterly motionless, sparkling like an ornament on the branch of a cosmic Christmas tree...
At the moment of our departure, Earth and Mars were on the same side of the sun. Even so, we had eighty-six million kilometers to travel...which would take us ninety-three days!
If you can call them "days"...
Since we were not rotating, the sun stood transfixed in the sky. It was always morning in the engine room, and night in the kitchen...
When our alarm clock decided that it was dawn, Sophie would calculate our precise position. I would correct our trajectory...
After splashing a little water on our faces, we would join Hans for breakfast.
...IF FOR NOTHING ELSE, IT'S GOOD TO HAVE AETHERITE!
YOU CAN SAY THAT AGAIN! WITHOUT ARTIFICIAL GRAVITY, GOOD LUCK COOKING SAUSAGES PROPERLY IN SPACE!
The rations used on polar expeditions worked well for us too.
Pemmican, lemon juice, dried meat...
Hans performed miracles with our limited provisions!
We carefully regulated water usage, but if the filtering system worked as planned, we would have sufficient reserves for ourselves and for the plants...We even had tomatoes!
Well, when the chamberlain chose to leave some for us.
IT'S TRUE, HE EATS LIKE A HORSE!
WE SHOULD HAVE BROUGHT A PIG INSTEAD—AT LEAST THERE'D BE A POINT TO FATTENING HIM UP!
OH, WELL...
I WARN YOU, IF THE ENGINES MALFUNCTION AND WE END UP ORBITING NEPTUNE, WE'RE GOING TO HAVE PÂTÉ OF CHAMBERLAIN FOR DINNER!

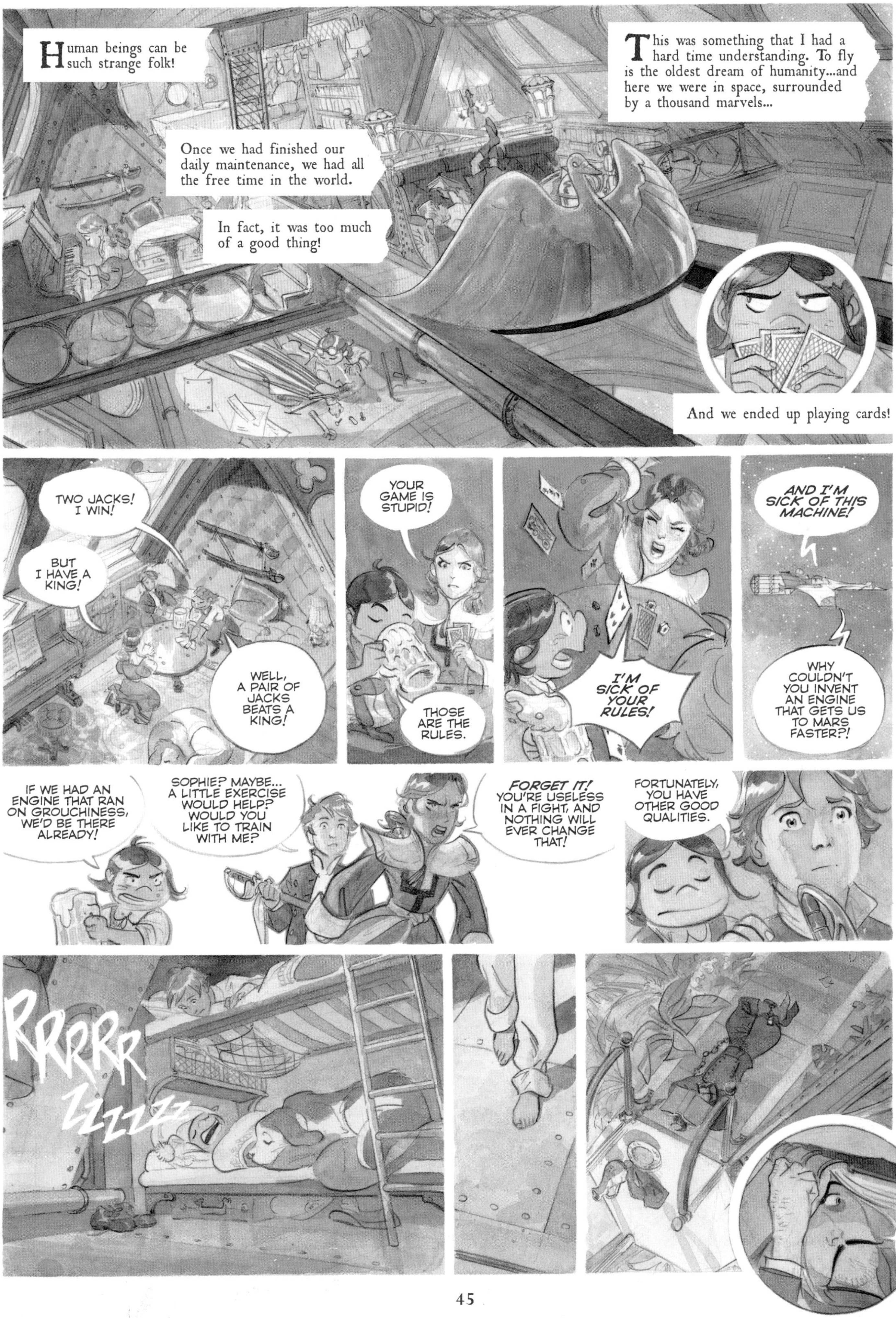
Human beings can be such strange folk!
This was something that I had a hard time understanding. To fly is the oldest dream of humanity...and here we were in space, surrounded by a thousand marvels...
Once we had finished our daily maintenance, we had all the free time in the world.
In fact, it was too much of a good thing!
And we ended up playing cards!
TWO JACKS! I WIN!
BUT I HAVE A KING!
WELL, A PAIR OF JACKS BEATS A KING!
YOUR GAME IS STUPID!
THOSE ARE THE RULES.
I'M SICK OF YOUR RULES!
AND I'M SICK OF THIS MACHINE!
WHY COULDN'T YOU INVENT AN ENGINE THAT GETS US TO MARS FASTER?!
IF WE HAD AN ENGINE THAT RAN ON GROUCHINESS, WE'D BE THERE ALREADY!
SOPHIE? MAYBE... A LITTLE EXERCISE WOULD HELP? WOULD YOU LIKE TO TRAIN WITH ME?
FORGET IT! YOU'RE USELESS IN A FIGHT, AND NOTHING WILL EVER CHANGE THAT!
FORTUNATELY, YOU HAVE OTHER GOOD QUALITIES.
RRRRR
ZZZZZZ
?

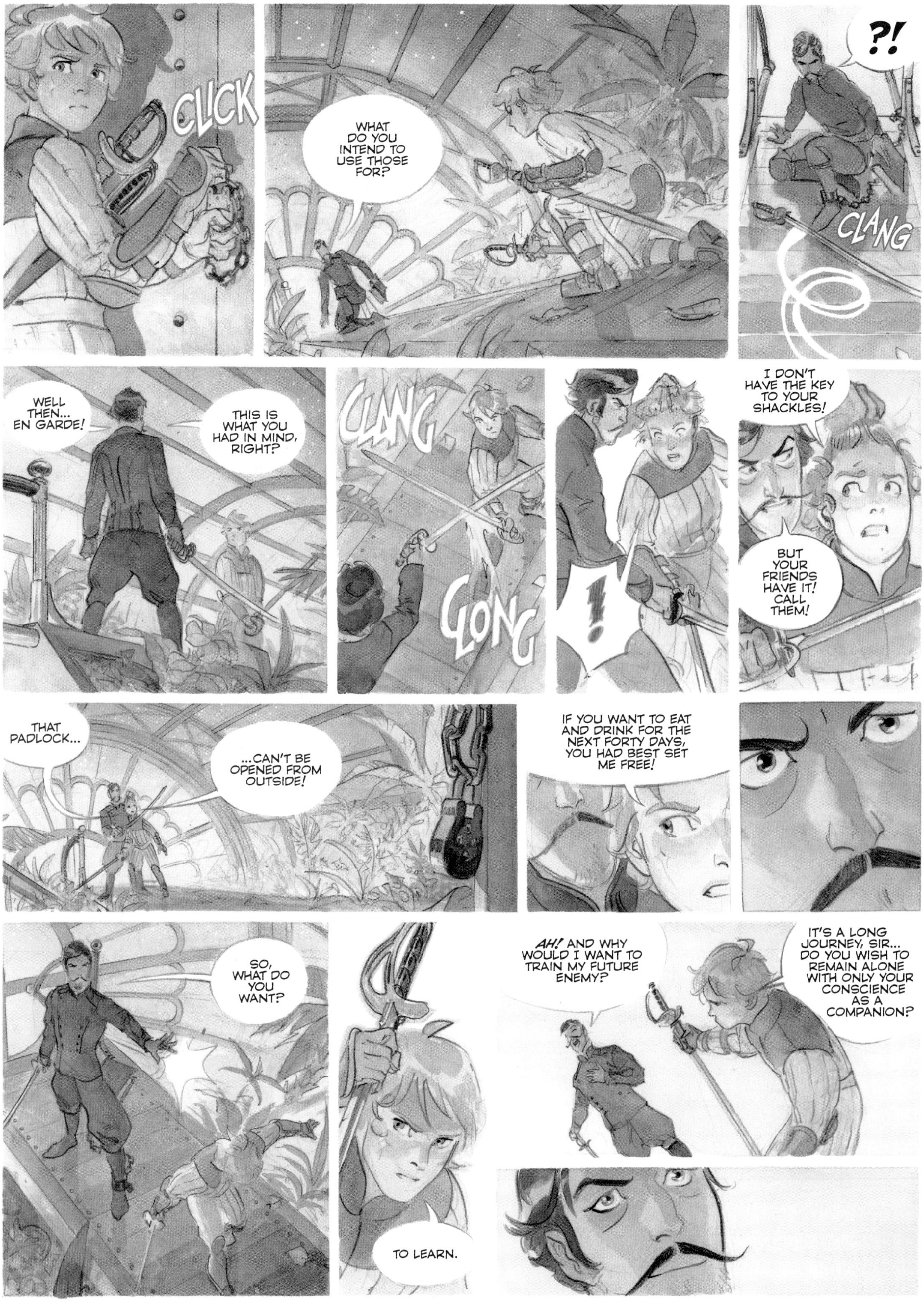
CLICK
WHAT DO YOU INTEND TO USE THOSE FOR?
?!
CLANG
WELL THEN... EN GARDE!
THIS IS WHAT YOU HAD IN MIND, RIGHT?
CLANG
CLONG
!
I DON'T HAVE THE KEY TO YOUR SHACKLES!
BUT YOUR FRIENDS HAVE IT! CALL THEM!
THAT PADLOCK...
...CAN'T BE OPENED FROM OUTSIDE!
IF YOU WANT TO EAT AND DRINK FOR THE NEXT FORTY DAYS, YOU HAD BEST SET ME FREE!
SO, WHAT DO YOU WANT?
TO LEARN.
AH! AND WHY WOULD I WANT TO TRAIN MY FUTURE ENEMY?
IT'S A LONG JOURNEY, SIR... DO YOU WISH TO REMAIN ALONE WITH ONLY YOUR CONSCIENCE AS A COMPANION?

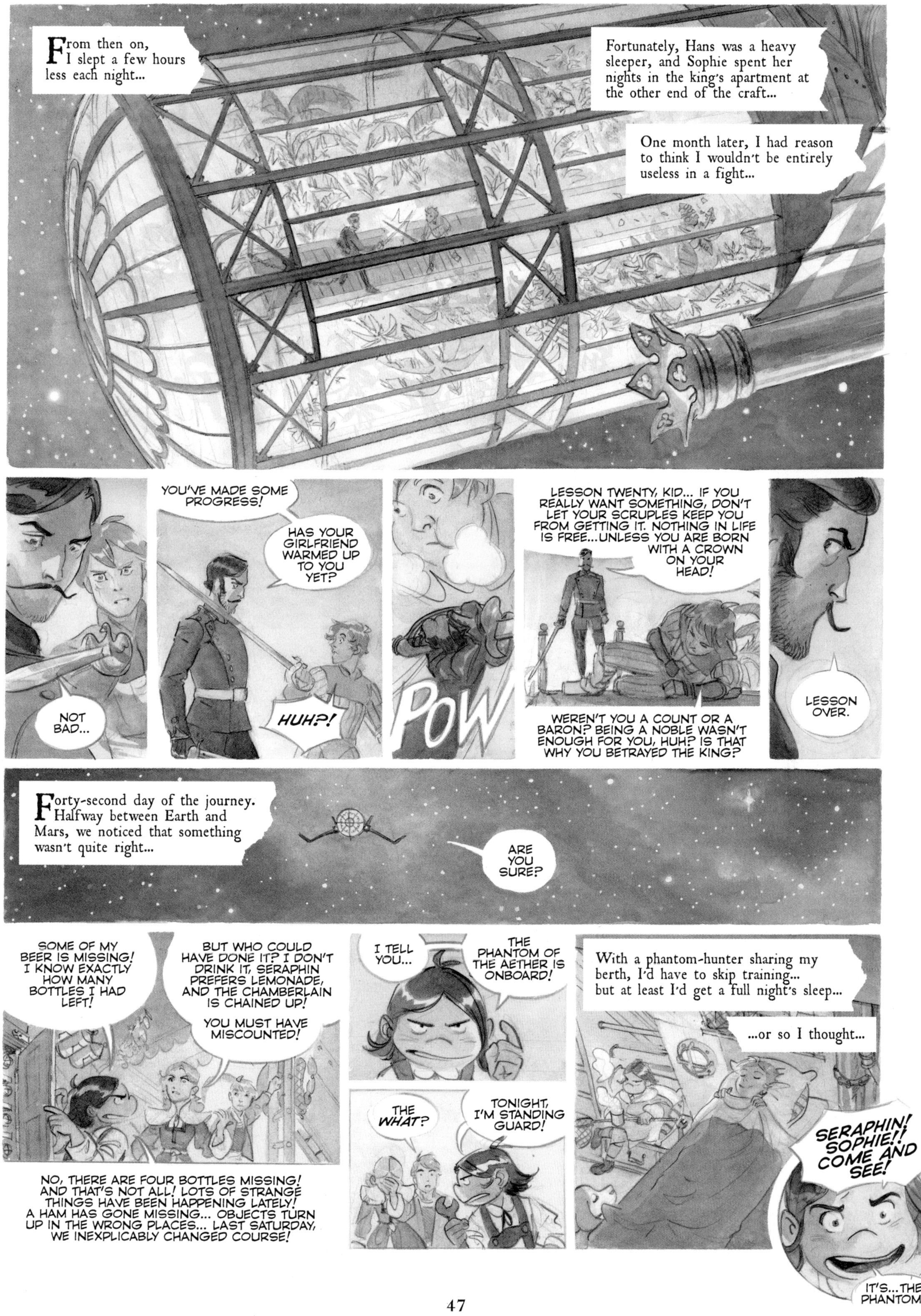
From then on, I slept a few hours less each night...
Fortunately, Hans was a heavy sleeper, and Sophie spent her nights in the king's apartment at the other end of the craft...
One month later, I had reason to think I wouldn't be entirely useless in a fight...
NOT BAD...
YOU'VE MADE SOME PROGRESS!
HAS YOUR GIRLFRIEND WARMED UP TO YOU YET?
HUH?!
POW
LESSON TWENTY, KID... IF YOU REALLY WANT SOMETHING, DON'T LET YOUR SCRUPLES KEEP YOU FROM GETTING IT. NOTHING IN LIFE IS FREE...UNLESS YOU ARE BORN WITH A CROWN ON YOUR HEAD!
WEREN'T YOU A COUNT OR A BARON? BEING A NOBLE WASN'T ENOUGH FOR YOU, HUH? IS THAT WHY YOU BETRAYED THE KING?
LESSON OVER.
Forty-second day of the journey. Halfway between Earth and Mars, we noticed that something wasn't quite right...
ARE YOU SURE?
SOME OF MY BEER IS MISSING! I KNOW EXACTLY HOW MANY BOTTLES I HAD LEFT!
BUT WHO COULD HAVE DONE IT? I DON'T DRINK IT, SERAPHIN PREFERS LEMONADE, AND THE CHAMBERLAIN IS CHAINED UP!
YOU MUST HAVE MISCOUNTED!
NO, THERE ARE FOUR BOTTLES MISSING! AND THAT'S NOT ALL! LOTS OF STRANGE THINGS HAVE BEEN HAPPENING LATELY! A HAM HAS GONE MISSING... OBJECTS TURN UP IN THE WRONG PLACES... LAST SATURDAY, WE INEXPLICABLY CHANGED COURSE!
I TELL YOU...
THE PHANTOM OF THE AETHER IS ONBOARD!
THE WHAT?
TONIGHT, I'M STANDING GUARD!
With a phantom-hunter sharing my berth, I'd have to skip training... but at least I'd get a full night's sleep...
...or so I thought...
SERAPHIN! SOPHIE!! COME AND SEE!
IT'S...THE PHANTOM!

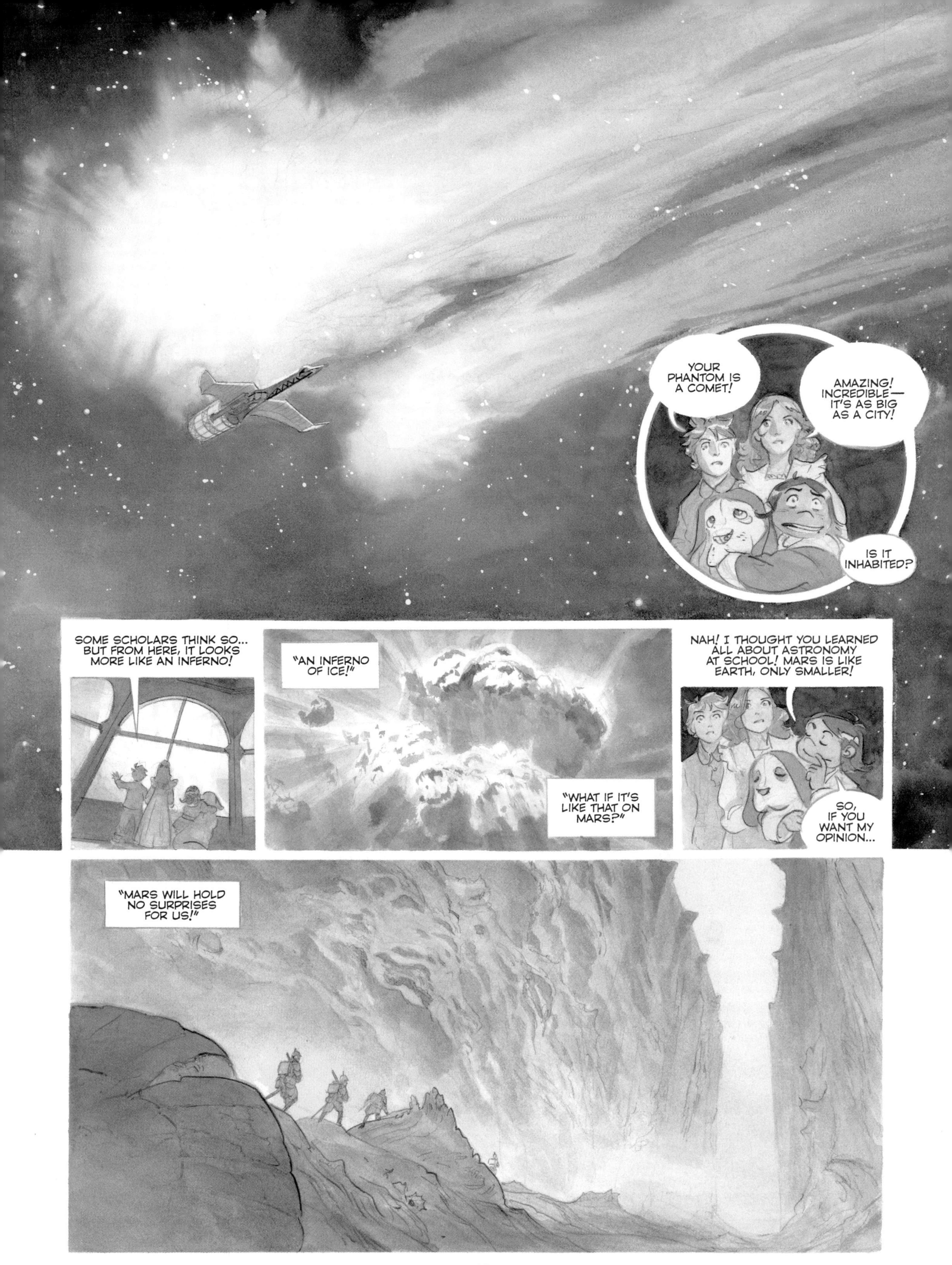
YOUR PHANTOM IS A COMET!
AMAZING! INCREDIBLE— IT'S AS BIG AS A CITY!
IS IT INHABITED?
SOME SCHOLARS THINK SO... BUT FROM HERE, IT LOOKS MORE LIKE AN INFERNO!
"AN INFERNO OF ICE!"
"WHAT IF IT'S LIKE THAT ON MARS?"
NAH! I THOUGHT YOU LEARNED ALL ABOUT ASTRONOMY AT SCHOOL! MARS IS LIKE EARTH, ONLY SMALLER!
SO, IF YOU WANT MY OPINION...
"MARS WILL HOLD NO SURPRISES FOR US!"

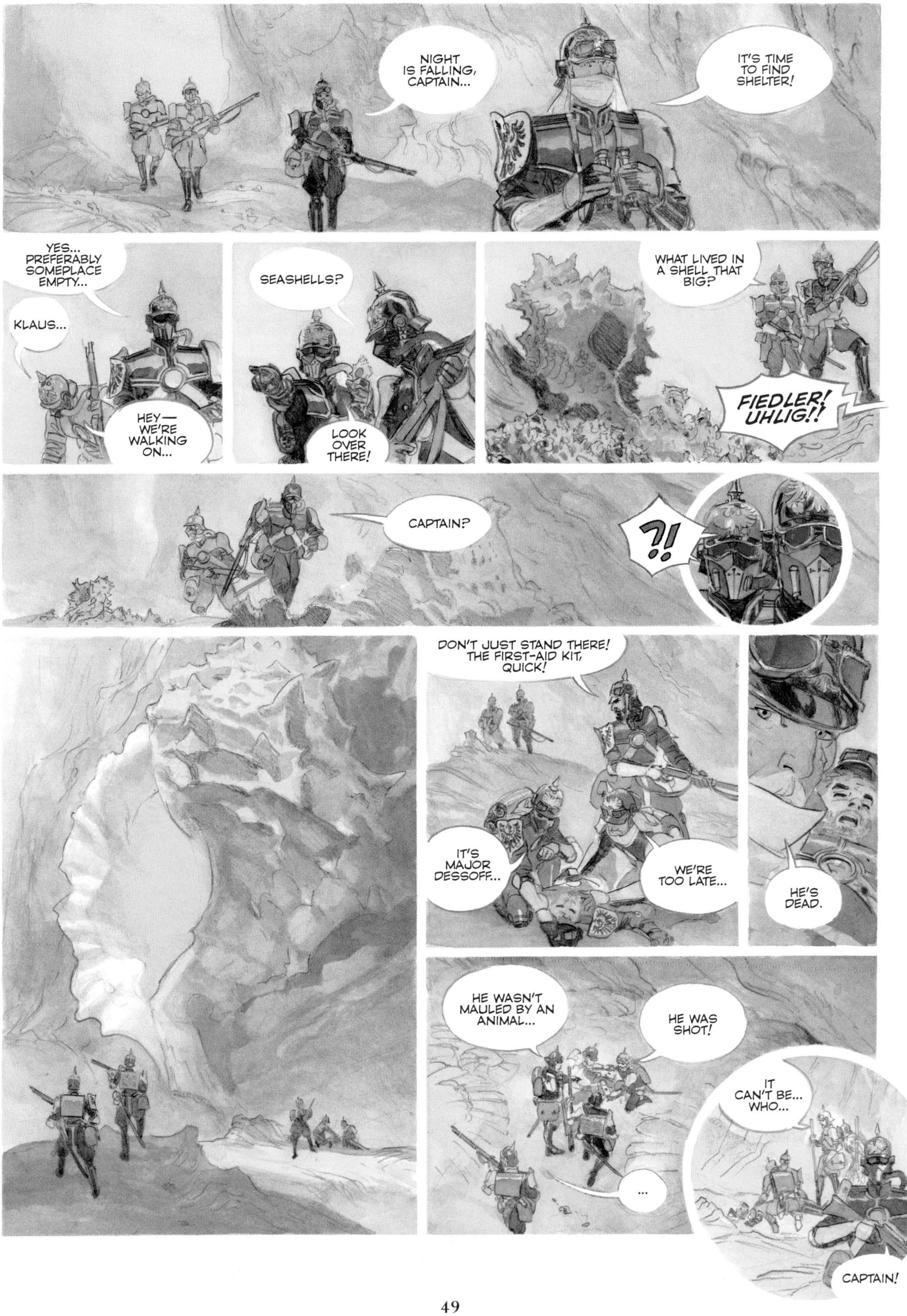
NIGHT IS FALLING, CAPTAIN...
IT'S TIME TO FIND SHELTER!
YES... PREFERABLY SOMEPLACE EMPTY...
KLAUS...
HEY— WE'RE WALKING ON...
SEASHELLS?
LOOK OVER THERE!
WHAT LIVED IN A SHELL THAT BIG?
FIEDLER! UHLIG!!
CAPTAIN?
?!
DON'T JUST STAND THERE! THE FIRST-AID KIT, QUICK!
IT'S MAJOR DESSOFF...
WE'RE TOO LATE...
HE'S DEAD.
HE WASN'T MAULED BY AN ANIMAL...
HE WAS SHOT!
...
IT CAN'T BE... WHO...
CAPTAIN!

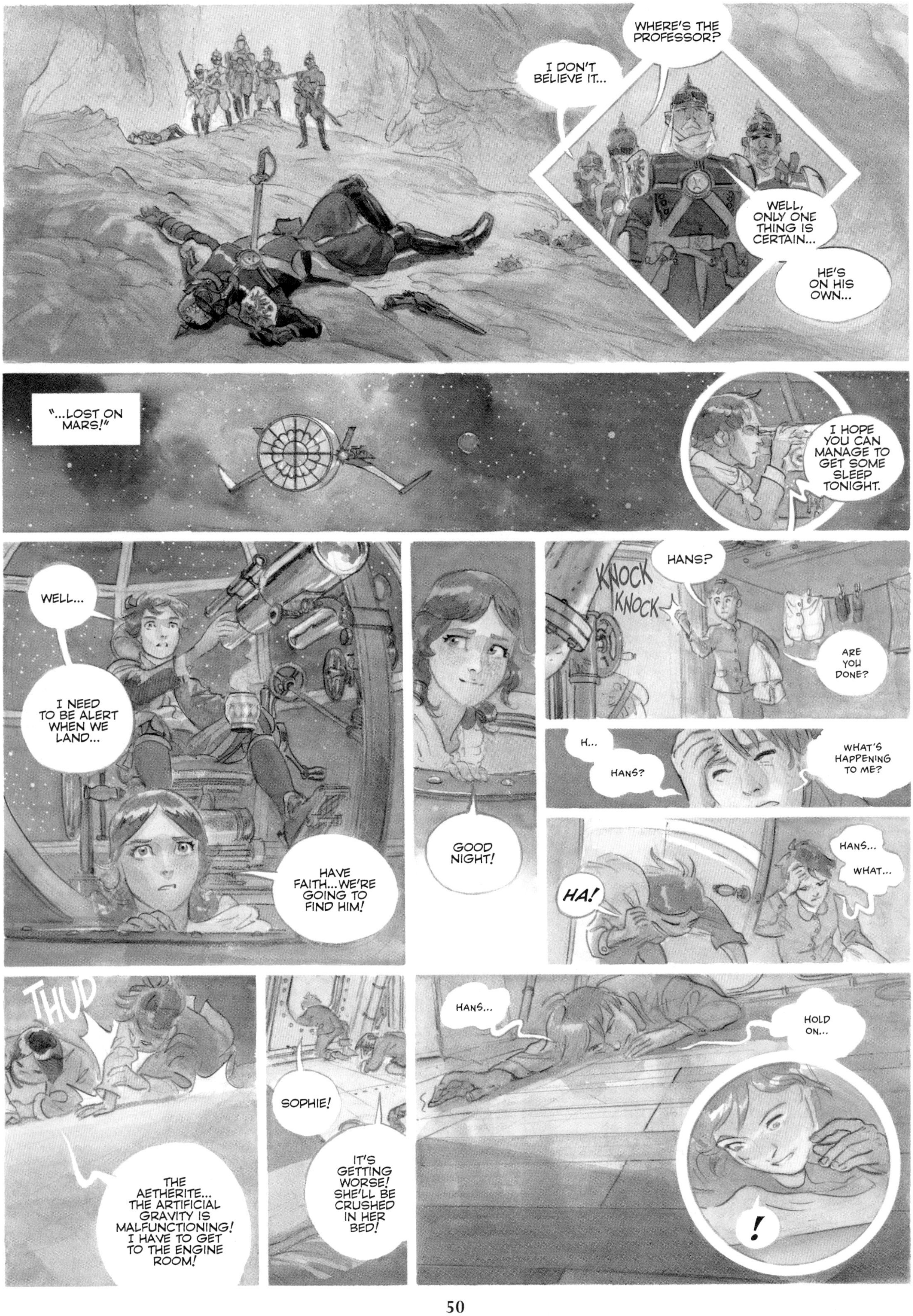
WHERE'S THE PROFESSOR?
I DON'T BELIEVE IT...
WELL, ONLY ONE THING IS CERTAIN...
HE'S ON HIS OWN...
"...LOST ON MARS!"
I HOPE YOU CAN MANAGE TO GET SOME SLEEP TONIGHT.
WELL...
I NEED TO BE ALERT WHEN WE LAND...
HAVE FAITH...WE'RE GOING TO FIND HIM!
GOOD NIGHT!
KNOCK KNOCK
HANS?
ARE YOU DONE?
H...
HANS?
WHAT'S HAPPENING TO ME?
HA!
HANS...
WHAT...
THUD
THE AETHERITE... THE ARTIFICIAL GRAVITY IS MALFUNCTIONING! I HAVE TO GET TO THE ENGINE ROOM!
SOPHIE!
IT'S GETTING WORSE! SHE'LL BE CRUSHED IN HER BED!
HANS...
HOLD ON...
!

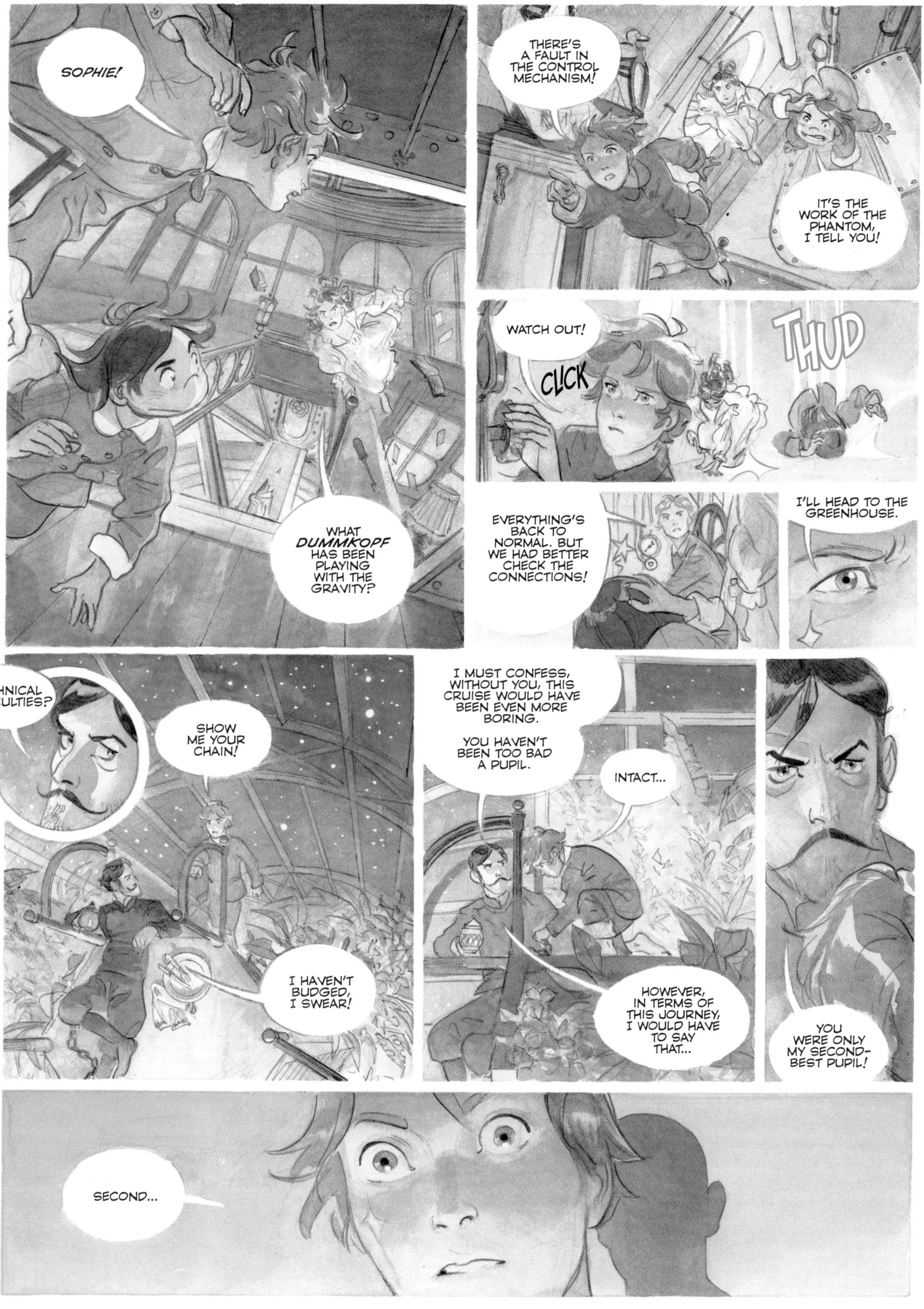
SOPHIE!
WHAT DUMMKOPF HAS BEEN PLAYING WITH THE GRAVITY?
THERE'S A FAULT IN THE CONTROL MECHANISM!
IT'S THE WORK OF THE PHANTOM, I TELL YOU!
WATCH OUT!
CLICK
THUD
EVERYTHING'S BACK TO NORMAL. BUT WE HAD BETTER CHECK THE CONNECTIONS!
I'LL HEAD TO THE GREENHOUSE.
TECHNICAL DIFFICULTIES?
SHOW ME YOUR CHAIN!
I HAVEN'T BUDGED, I SWEAR!
I MUST CONFESS, WITHOUT YOU, THIS CRUISE WOULD HAVE BEEN EVEN MORE BORING.
YOU HAVEN'T BEEN TOO BAD A PUPIL.
INTACT...
HOWEVER, IN TERMS OF THIS JOURNEY, I WOULD HAVE TO SAY THAT...
YOU WERE ONLY MY SECOND-BEST PUPIL!
SECOND...

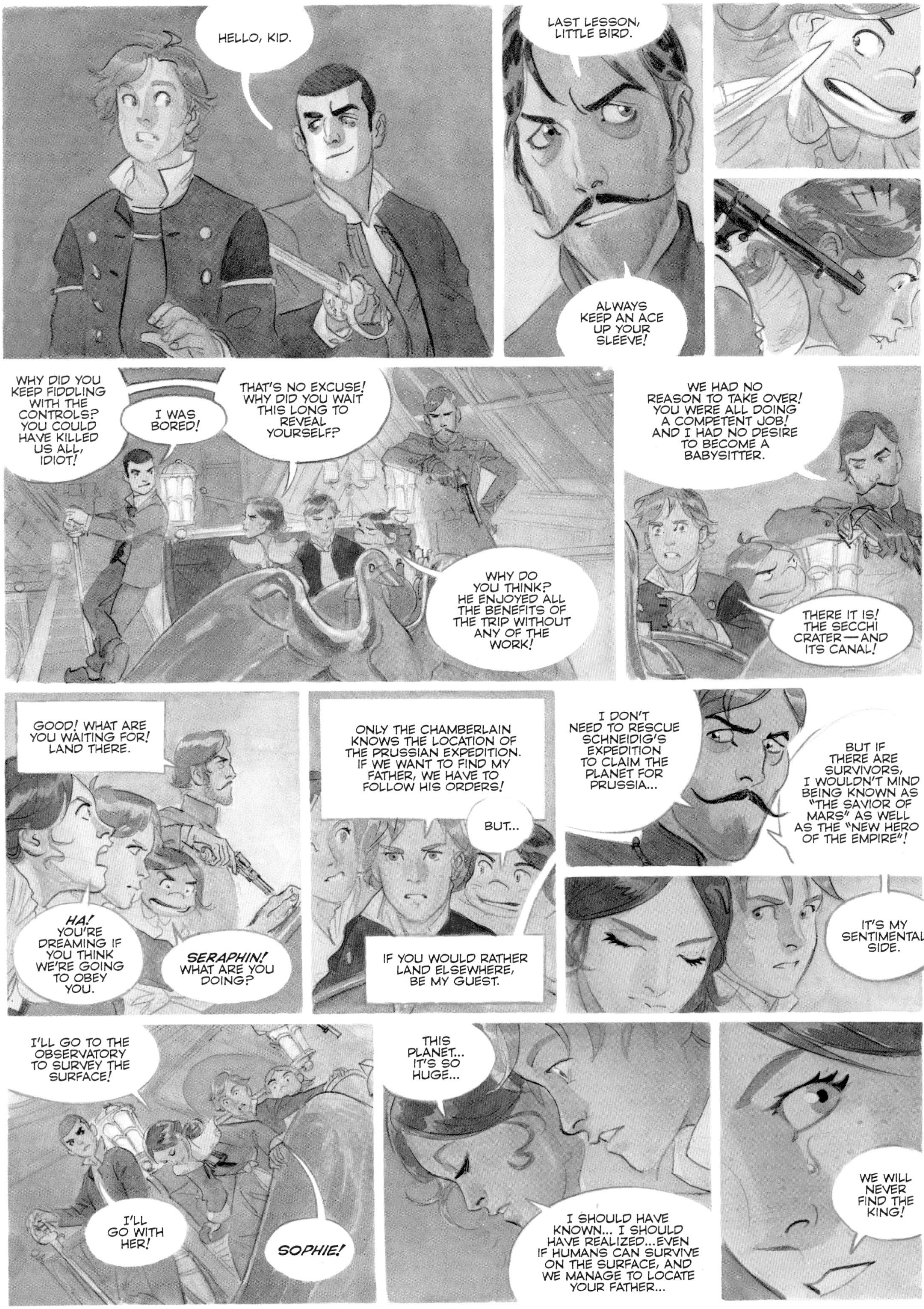

HELLO, KID.
LAST LESSON, LITTLE BIRD.
ALWAYS KEEP AN ACE UP YOUR SLEEVE!
WHY DID YOU KEEP FIDDLING WITH THE CONTROLS? YOU COULD HAVE KILLED US ALL, IDIOT!
I WAS BORED!
THAT'S NO EXCUSE! WHY DID YOU WAIT THIS LONG TO REVEAL YOURSELF?
WHY DO YOU THINK? HE ENJOYED ALL THE BENEFITS OF THE TRIP WITHOUT ANY OF THE WORK!
WE HAD NO REASON TO TAKE OVER! YOU WERE ALL DOING A COMPETENT JOB! AND I HAD NO DESIRE TO BECOME A BABYSITTER.
THERE IT IS! THE SECCHI CRATER—AND ITS CANAL!
GOOD! WHAT ARE YOU WAITING FOR! LAND THERE.
HA! YOU'RE DREAMING IF YOU THINK WE'RE GOING TO OBEY YOU.
SERAPHIN! WHAT ARE YOU DOING?
ONLY THE CHAMBERLAIN KNOWS THE LOCATION OF THE PRUSSIAN EXPEDITION. IF WE WANT TO FIND MY FATHER, WE HAVE TO FOLLOW HIS ORDERS!
BUT...
IF YOU WOULD RATHER LAND ELSEWHERE, BE MY GUEST.
I DON'T NEED TO RESCUE SCHNEIDIG'S EXPEDITION TO CLAIM THE PLANET FOR PRUSSIA...
BUT IF THERE ARE SURVIVORS, I WOULDN'T MIND BEING KNOWN AS "THE SAVIOR OF MARS" AS WELL AS THE "NEW HERO OF THE EMPIRE"!
IT'S MY SENTIMENTAL SIDE.
I'LL GO TO THE OBSERVATORY TO SURVEY THE SURFACE!
I'LL GO WITH HER!
SOPHIE!
THIS PLANET... IT'S SO HUGE...
I SHOULD HAVE KNOWN... I SHOULD HAVE REALIZED... EVEN IF HUMANS CAN SURVIVE ON THE SURFACE, AND WE MANAGE TO LOCATE YOUR FATHER...
WE WILL NEVER FIND THE KING!

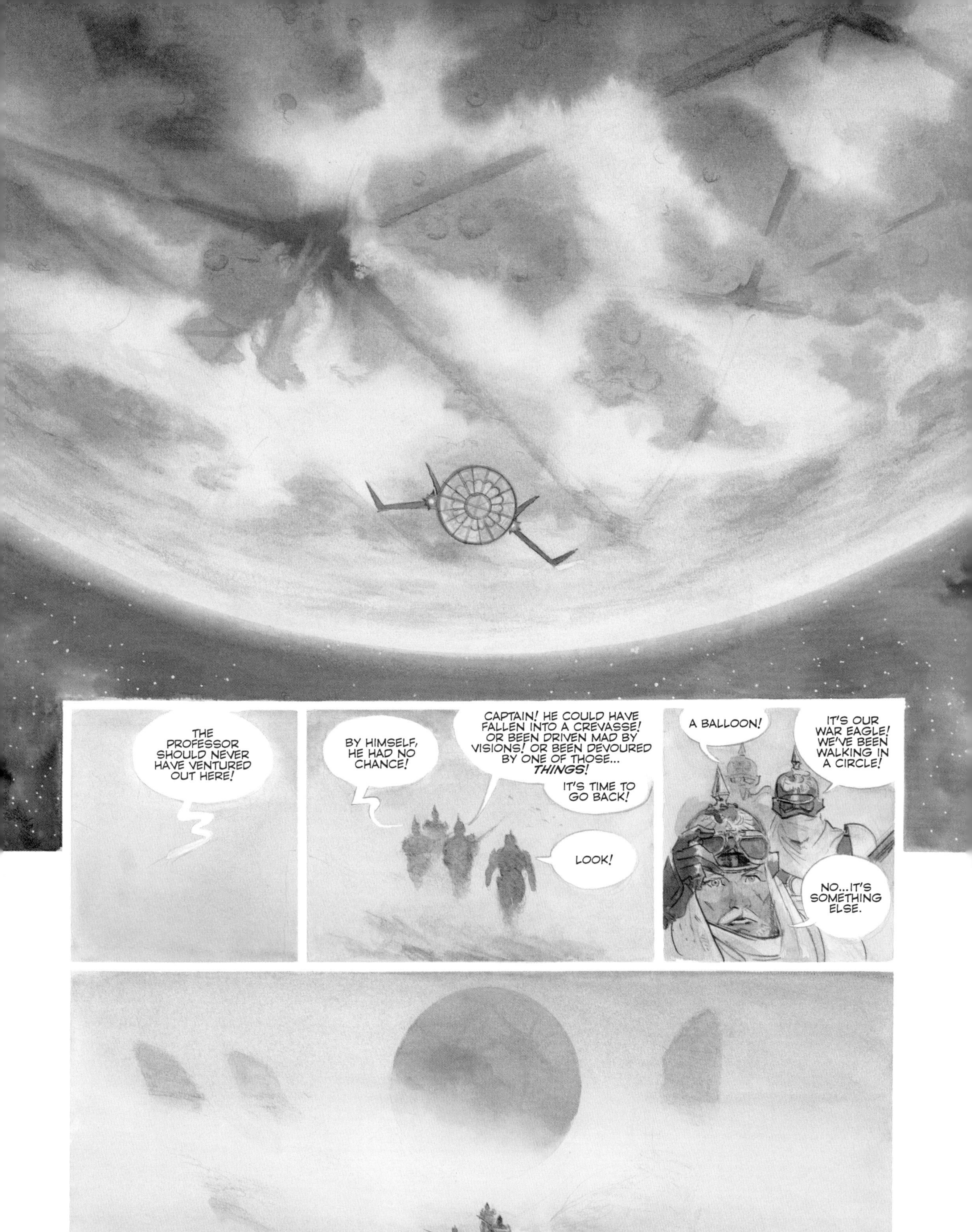
THE PROFESSOR SHOULD NEVER HAVE VENTURED OUT HERE!
BY HIMSELF, HE HAD NO CHANCE!
CAPTAIN! HE COULD HAVE FALLEN INTO A CREVASSE! OR BEEN DRIVEN MAD BY VISIONS! OR BEEN DEVOURED BY ONE OF THOSE... THINGS!
IT'S TIME TO GO BACK!
LOOK!
A BALLOON!
IT'S OUR WAR EAGLE! WE'VE BEEN WALKING IN A CIRCLE!
NO...IT'S SOMETHING ELSE.

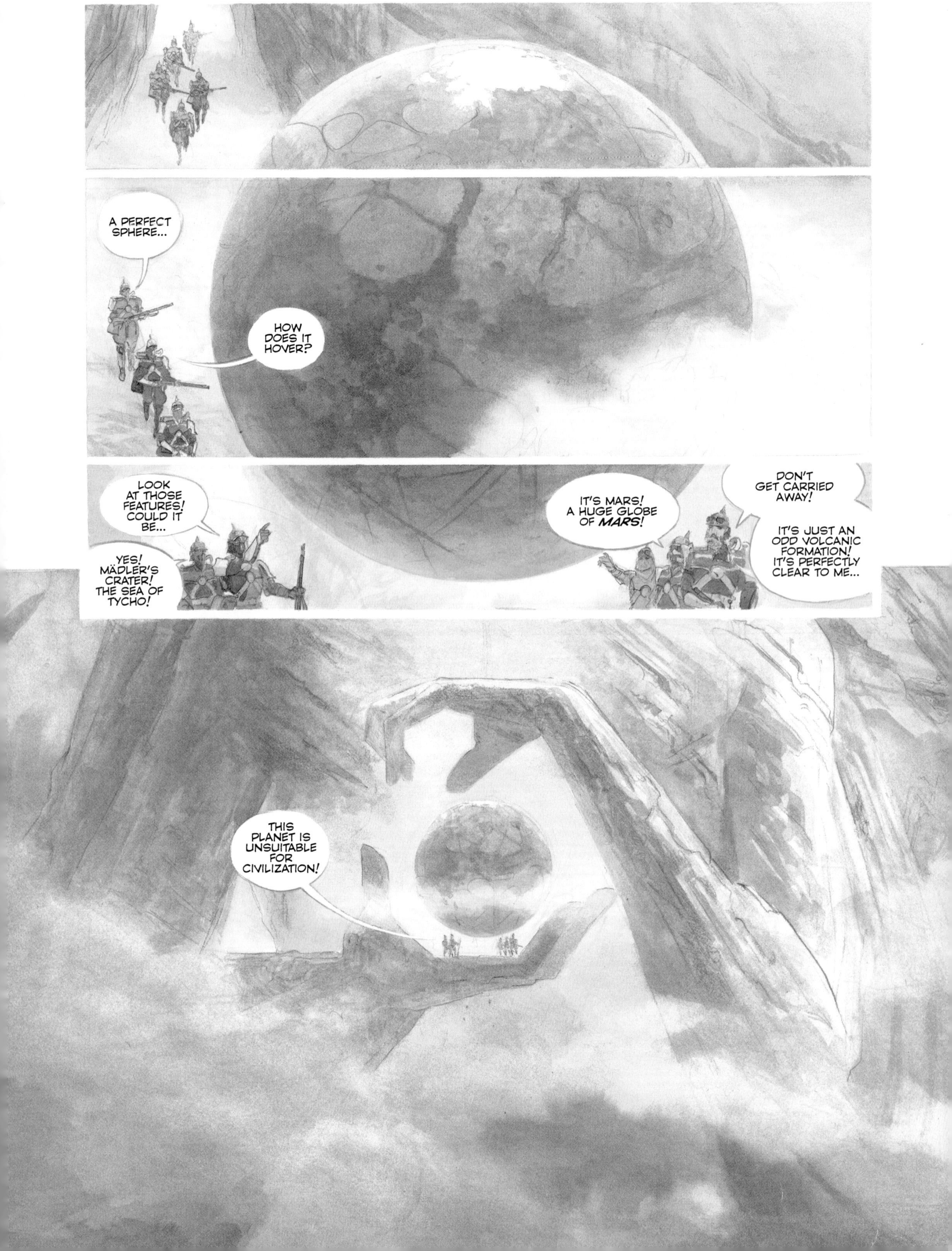
A PERFECT SPHERE...
HOW DOES IT HOVER?
LOOK AT THOSE FEATURES! COULD IT BE...
YES! MÄDLER'S CRATER! THE SEA OF TYCHO!
IT'S MARS! A HUGE GLOBE OF MARS!
DON'T GET CARRIED AWAY!
IT'S JUST AN ODD VOLCANIC FORMATION! IT'S PERFECTLY CLEAR TO ME...
THIS PLANET IS UNSUITABLE FOR CIVILIZATION!

# TO BE CONTINUED IN

# CASTLE
## IN
## THE
# STARS

### A FRENCHMAN ON MARS

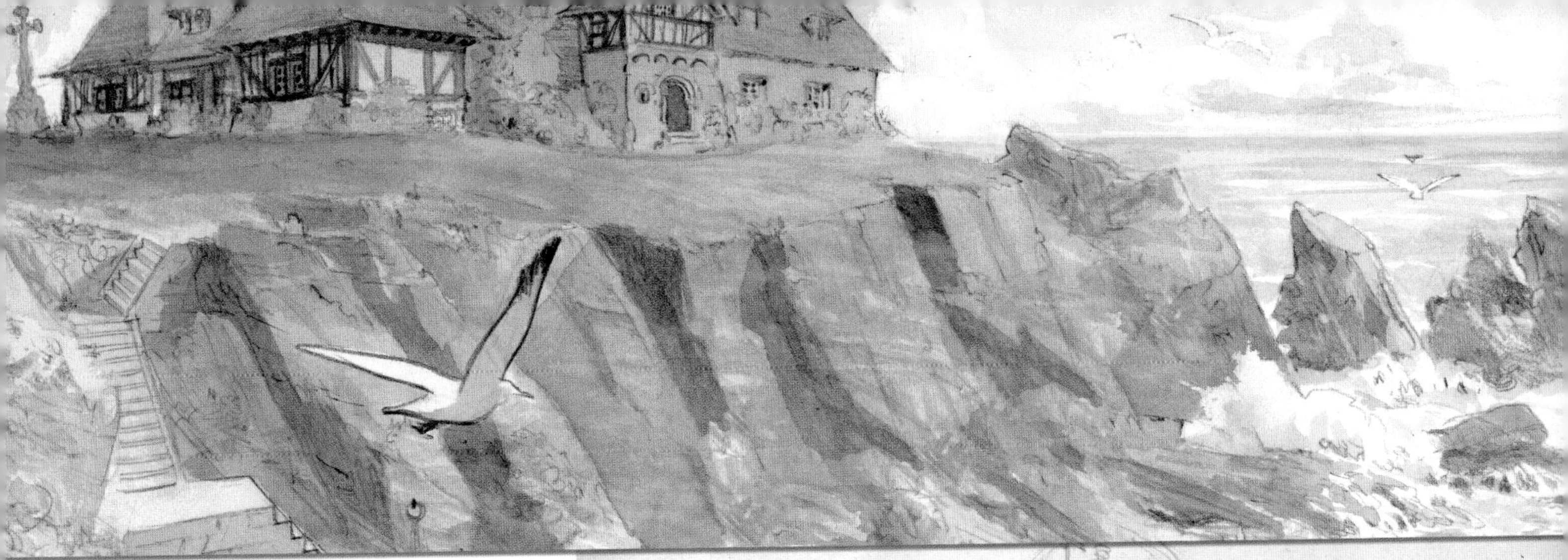

# THE ART OF

# CASTLE IN THE STARS

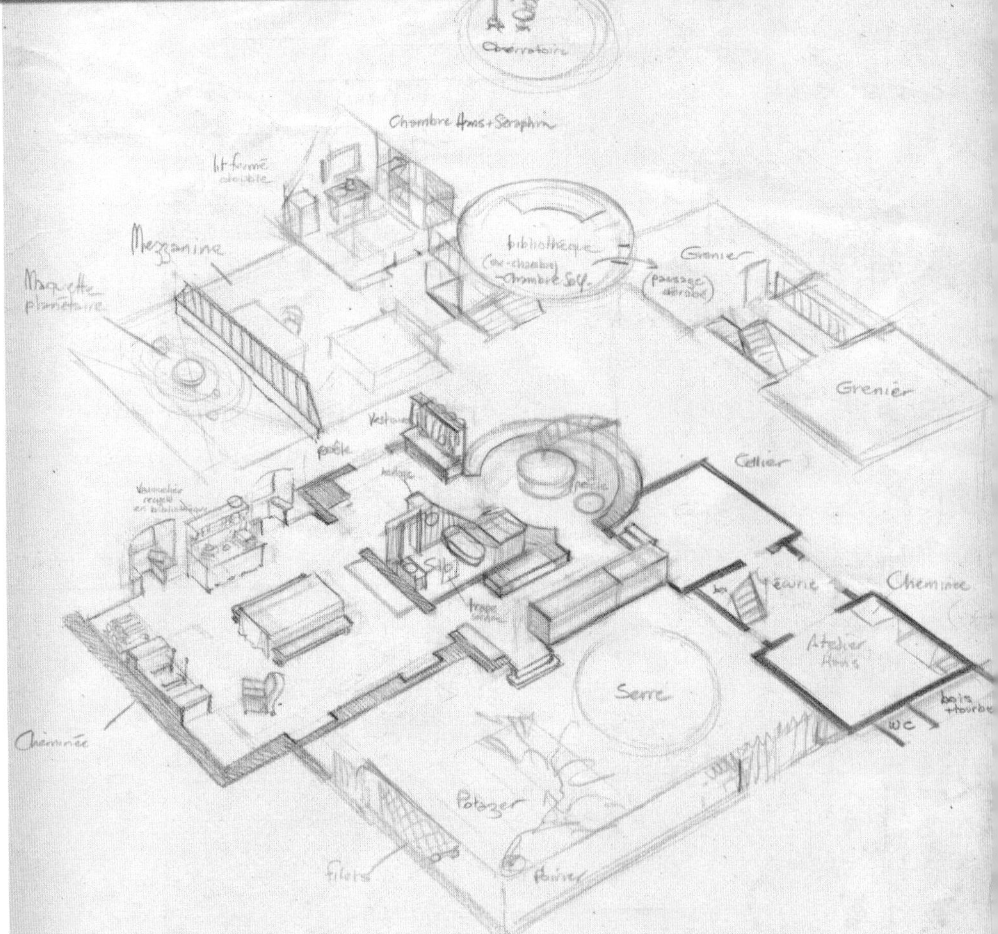
Observatoire
Chambre Hans+Seraphin
Mezzanine
Maquette planétaire
bibliothèque
Grenier
Grenier
Cellier
Chéminée
Chéminée
Atelier Hans
Serre
Potager
Poirier
filets

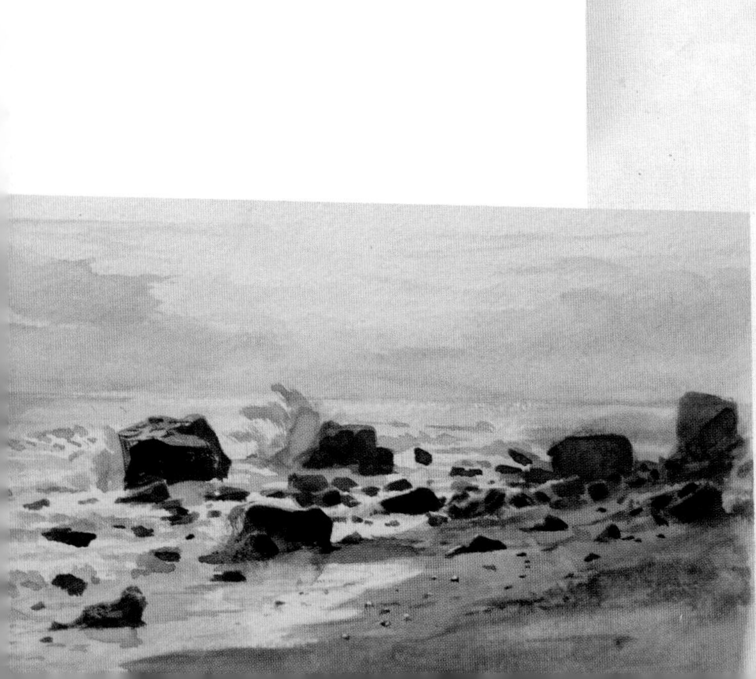

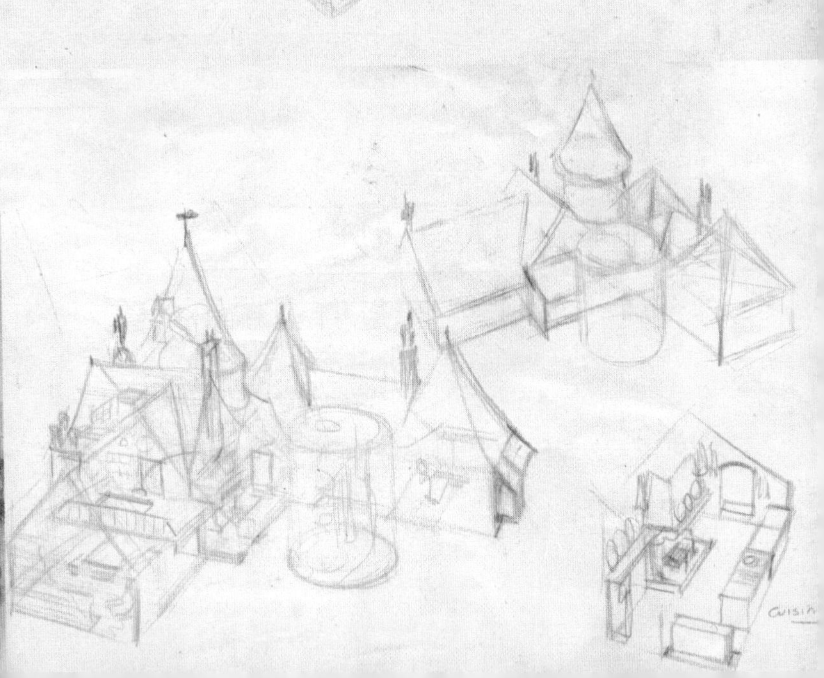
Cuisine

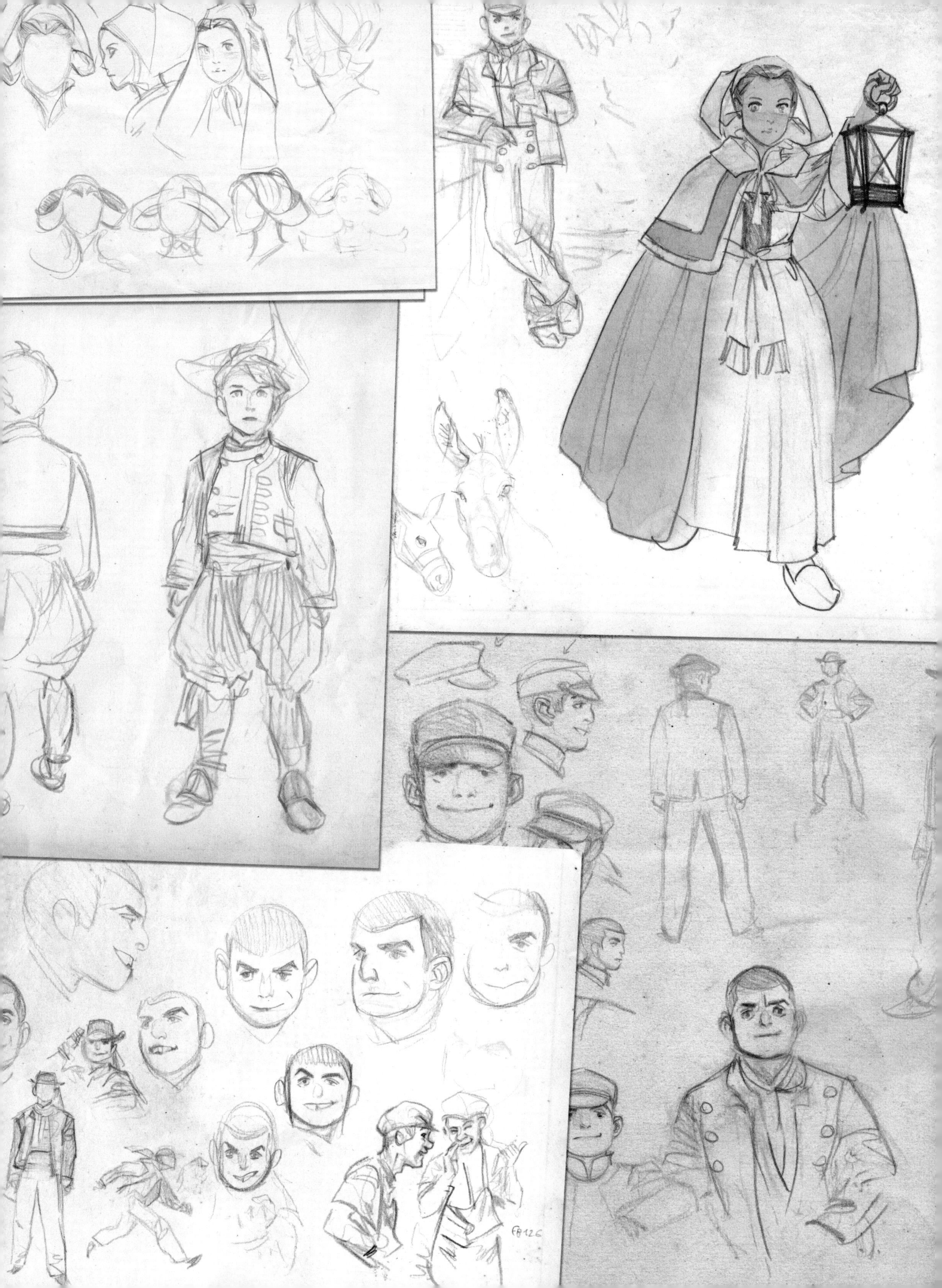
FB 126

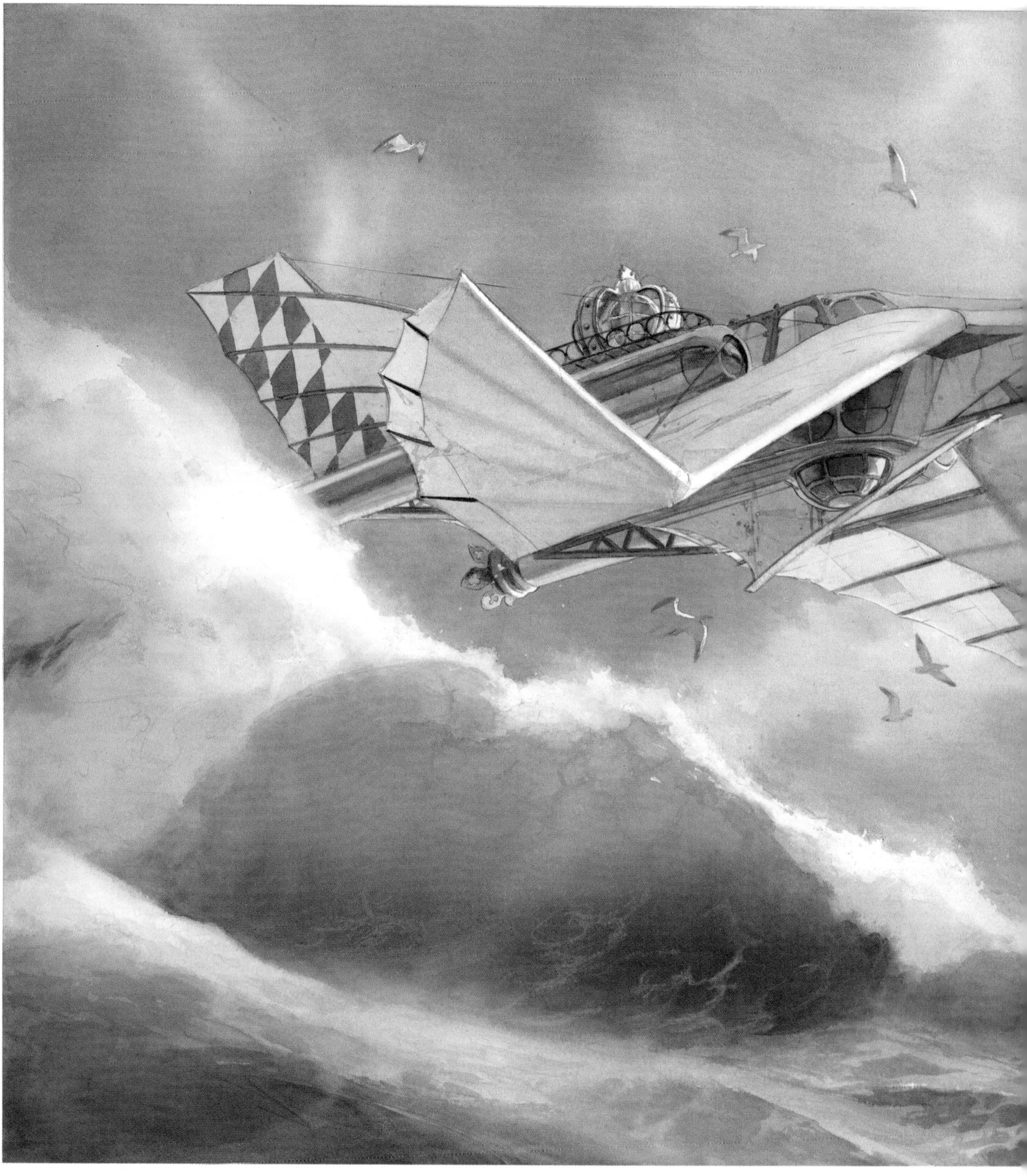

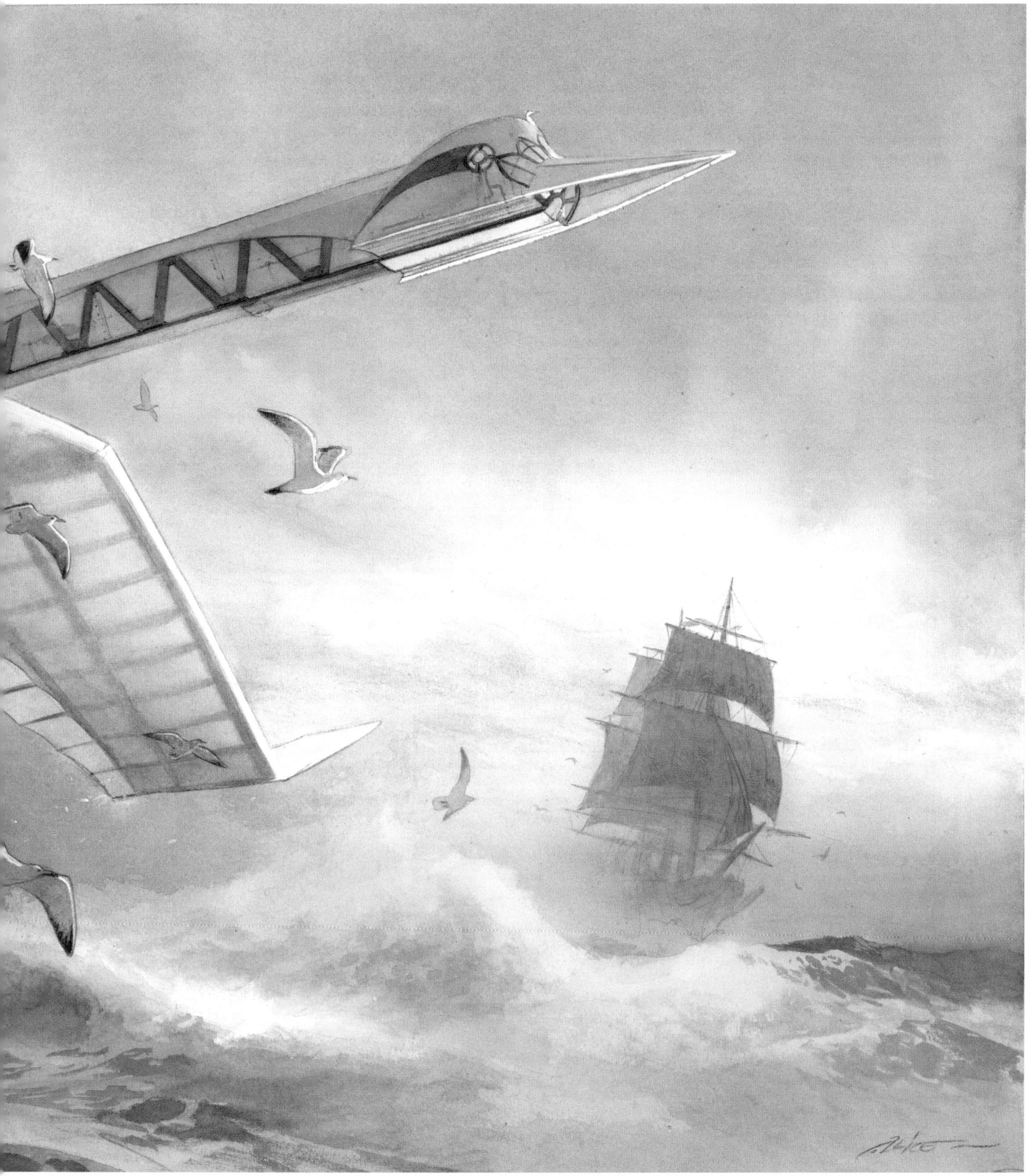

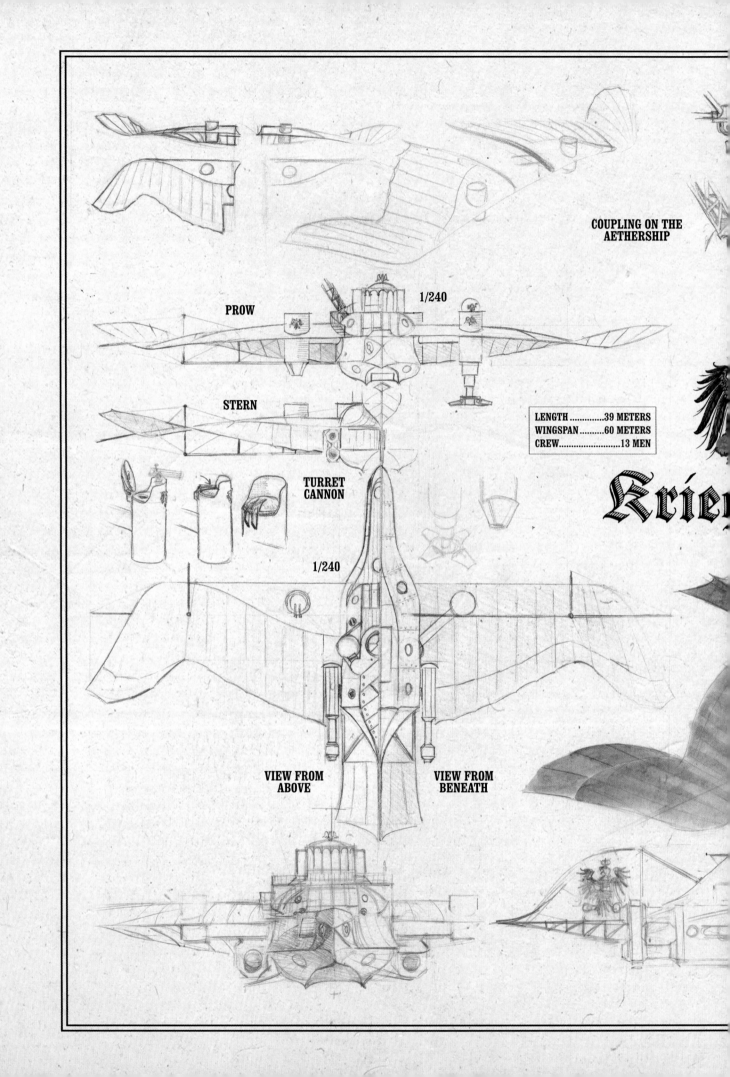

COUPLING ON THE
AETHERSHIP

PROW

1/240

STERN

LENGTH ...............39 METERS
WINGSPAN ..........60 METERS
CREW.......................13 MEN

TURRET
CANNON

Krien

1/240

VIEW FROM
ABOVE

VIEW FROM
BENEATH

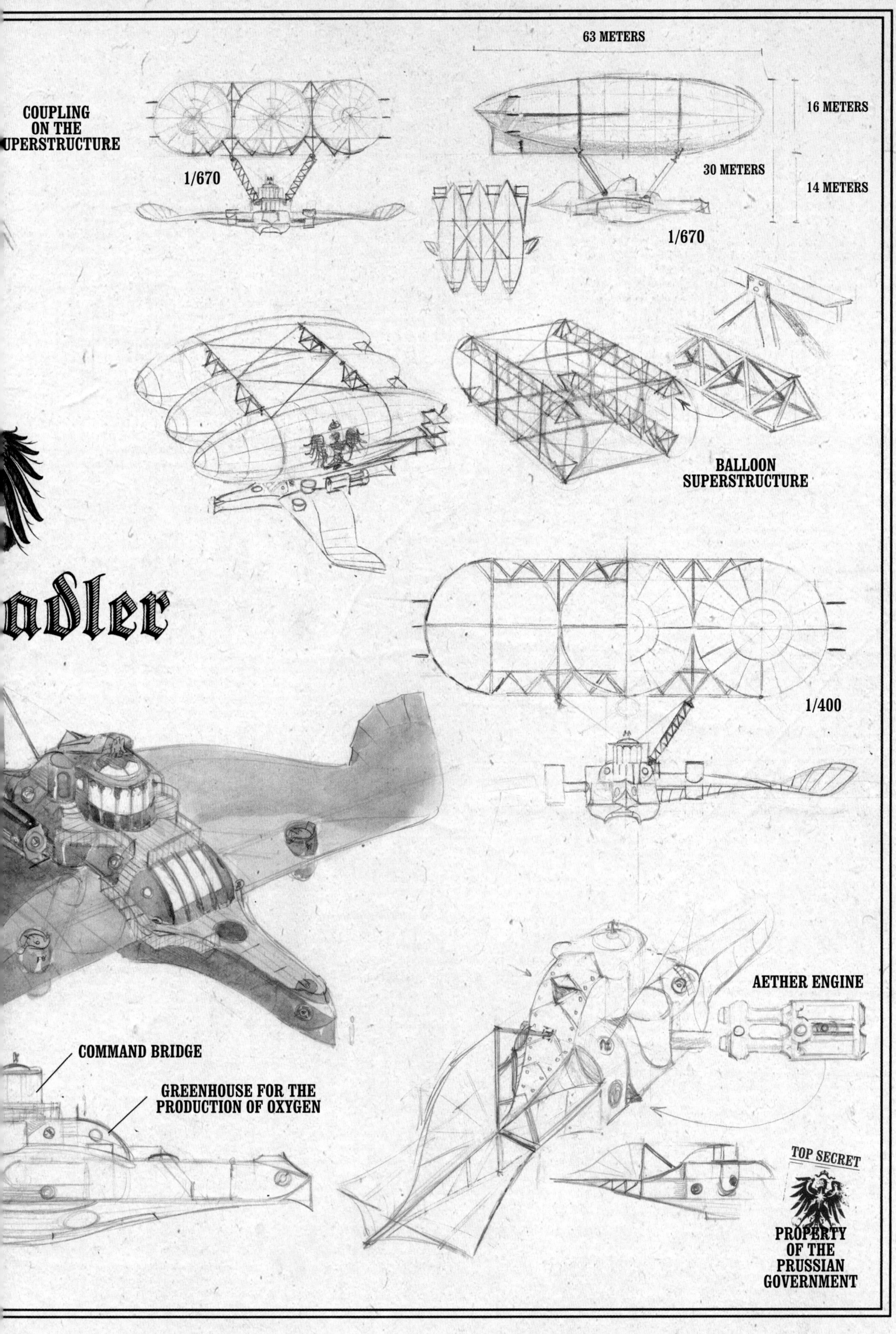
63 METERS
COUPLING
ON THE
UPERSTRUCTURE
1/670
16 METERS
30 METERS
14 METERS
1/670
BALLOON
SUPERSTRUCTURE
adler
1/400
AETHER ENGINE
COMMAND BRIDGE
GREENHOUSE FOR THE
PRODUCTION OF OXYGEN
TOP SECRET
PROPERTY
OF THE
PRUSSIAN
GOVERNMENT

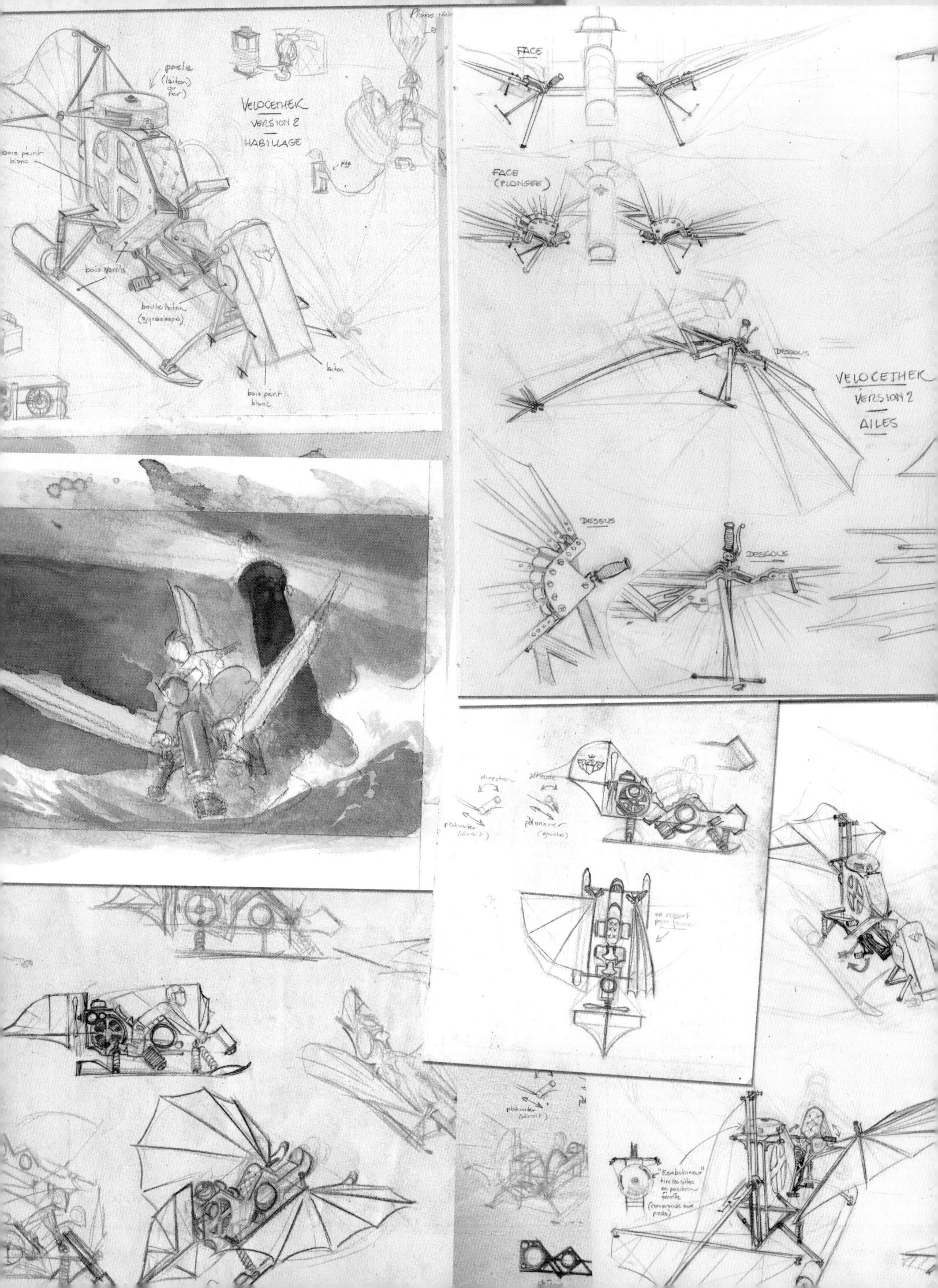
poele
(laiton
ou
fer)
VELOCETHER
VERSION 2
HABILLAGE
bois peint
blanc
bois vernis
boule laiton
(gyroscope)
laiton
bois peint
blanc
pile
FACE
FACE
(PLONGEE)
DESSOUS
VELOCETHER
VERSION 2
AILES
DESSUS
DESSOUS
direction
altitude
palonnier
(droit)
palonnier
(gauche)
palonnier
(droit)
"Rembobineur"
tire les ailes
en position
fermée
(commande aux
pieds)